Struck By Lightning
and other bolts of reality

Cyd Webster Beacham

Son of a Covet *co-authored by George Ward Beacham III*

To Sis Boyd,
Be blessed!
Cyndie
10/14/14

ISBN-10: 0989280519
ISBN-13: 978-0-9892805-1-8

Because of the dynamic nature of the Internet, any Web addresses or links contained in this book may have changed since publication and may no longer be valid. The expressed in this work are solely those of the authors.

Dedication

To my mom, Elaine Webster, who—even posthumously—never let me forget about "writing that book."

Acknowledgements

I am so grateful to my Lord and Savior, Jesus Christ for every breath I take. I wake up saying 'Thank You' every morning and rejoice because I am a living testimony of God's grace and mercy. I have so many family members and friends who have been very encouraging and supportive of my writing journey, especially my husband, George Beacham, who co-authored the new story in this second printing— *Son of a Covet*. Thank you to Lloyd D. Henderson, Esq. for contributing with forward comments. Thank you to Shirley Hendricks, Gail Purnell and my brother LeRoy 'Lee' Webster for your reviews and assistance.

The popularity of *Struck By Lightning and other bolts of reality* is very inspiring. I have received many comments from people who have read the stories in this book, who identify with some of scenarios and characters, personally, or by knowing people who live in dysfunction. Readers may come away with an understanding that it is possible to change when surrender, self-reflection and courage to make choices to love oneself, are achieved. Redemption and overcoming legacies of trauma and low self-esteem empower some to make choices that can lead to triumph, comfort and peace.

Thank you to my family and friends for keeping me grounded and sharing in my enthusiasm as I continue my writing journey.

'Happiness is a choice!'

Author's Note

This book is a novel expression of relief and an acknowledgement of the human experience as I have experienced it and imagined it. All stories are fictitious, and any resemblance to real people and places is purely coincidental.

Forward

In the short story, Son of a Covet, delivers an interesting demonstration of how a family's generational history served as a blueprint for Roman's behavior without him even being fully conscious of it.

Far too many of us have a family history deeply rooted in dysfunctional behavioral patterns. Although some of our behavioral patterns, which many believe are inherited from generation to generation, can be beneficial-valuing hard work or education.

Unfortunately, there are also negative/destructive patterns ranging from a history of violence, divorce to even some addictions. While an individual's family history of dysfunctional behavioral patterns are seemingly uncontrollable, what can be controlled are the decisions and choices one makes in terms of breaking the destructive cycle and creating a new positive family heritage for future descendants.

Lloyd D. Henderson, Esq.
President
Camden County East NAACP
PO Box 53
Lawnside, NJ 08045

*"All human actions have one or more of these seven causes:
chance, nature, compulsion, habit, reason, passion, and desire."
Aristotle*

Contents

Son of a Covet

1

"Look Pastor, I hear what you're saying but you don't understand my situation. I think it's best that you mind your business".

Roman Knox sat forward in his chair putting emphasis on his defiance. He leaned in as he spoke as if he were going to stand up, but didn't. While teetering on the edge of the chair, he waited for Pastor Stiles to say something, but instead the pastor just stared at him, and finally let out an audible sigh.

"You're making a big mistake Roman. You know I've counseled many people, thousands actually. You're making a mistake. And I think you know it deep down, but you're letting your emotions cloud your thinking."

"My marriage has been over. My fiancé..."

"Fiancé? You have the nerve to consider yourself engaged while still married to your wife? Just stop. Please stop and think about what you're doing. I agree that you need to get divorced. But you need to wait until after you're divorced before jumping into another relationship. You need a period to regroup, to settle down with yourself. Start focusing on God and pray. Get involved in some ministries and take your mind off of this obsession to be in a relationship. Do some self-reflection— and THEN— then, after some time has passed— at least a year, then think about dating."

Roman looked at his watch before the Pastor did this time, and stood up even though there was still almost 15 more minutes to go for the appointment.

"You don't know what you're talking about" Roman said as he headed for the door. "I've got somewhere to go, so uh... bye" and out the door he went, and calmly walked out the church greeting people as he made his way to his car.

As he drove out of the parking lot, he began to think about his conversation with Pastor Stiles and began mumbling out loud, "He don't know what he's talking about. My marriage has been over. She knows it. So technically, I HAVE waited before getting into another relationship. As far as I'm concerned, my marriage has been over long before I met Neesha."

Roman had turned left out of the parking lot without even thinking about it, as if he were heading toward his wife's home. He had been referring to it as his wife's home once he began spending nights with Neesha more frequently. It was maybe three or four months after meeting Neesha, that he stopped sleeping at his home where his wife lives altogether. So he continued on driving in that direction, deciding that he may as well stop by there and pick up a few things to bring to Neesha's, where he really lives.

"What are you doing here?" Ethel shouted in a startled voice as Roman came through the door. She had been meaning to change the locks and made a mental note to do that first thing the next day. "Don't be coming in here like that. You need to ring the doorbell or call first."

"This is still my house. I need to pick up some things... stop trippin'..."

"What are you doing around here anyway?" she asked sounding very annoyed.

"I met with Pastor Stiles... He wanted to meet with me after you showed him that picture. I done told you about putting our business out in the street..."

"I didn't put our business in the street. I spoke to the Pastor like I should have done long ago. I just don't understand you. What did I do that was so wrong? That we can't recover... You have a son here..."

"Leave him out of this. That's YOUR son. I tried to be a father to him but you had a problem with that. And, on top of that, you started talking to me like you talk to your son— yelling at me and carrying on like I'm your child... No. I've had enough of that. I was going to file for divorce before— months ago. But when my mom got sick, everything went on hold. Now that she's gone, I'm moving forward with my plans."

8

"Roman, please. Can't we sit down and talk about this? You're not thinking straight with all you've been through with your mother".

"No. I'm done talking." He went into their bedroom and snatched the closet door open to get his suit and a few other things. Then he headed toward the door without bothering to look at her, nor did he bother to say goodbye as he walked out, mumbling about how he needs to put her out and change the locks.

When he arrived at Neesha's house, he sat in his car in the driveway and began to think about his meeting with Pastor Stiles. He put his head back and huffed out a deep exhale, and drifted off to sleep.

It was a steamy, very warm day— the kind of day that made everyone and everything feel damp, inside and outside of the mansion. Roman had risen earlier than usual this morning judging by the darkness with a hint of light edging the lower horizon.

"Anotha damp, humid day" he mumbled as he placed his feet on the cool floor and braced himself to stand his achy body upright.

"Umph! Ugh!" He grunted as he stood up and stretched his arms to the ceiling. "Thank you Lawd for allowin' me anotha day hyeah. I'm askin' fer patience an understandin' ta hep me do a good job fo' Massa Aiken. An bless he an family too. An bless my chillins too."

Roman went thru his morning ritual of washing up and getting dressed in his butler's uniform and made his way upstairs into the kitchen to eat his breakfast before standing at his post in the front foyer as the house greeter and assistant to their owner, Master Aiken.

"Why you go an tell Sallie you ain't marryin her? She done had three a yourn' chillins..."

"Hush up woman and git me my breakfis. I done tole you an Sallie too. It don't make no sense ta go through marryin' as no slave. I know Massa Aiken might probly accep'it, but what good it do? She gots chillins by he an' me. An anyway, I done tole y'all I have a wife..."

"You ain't never gonna see her agin and ya knows it. She sold many years ago— she an yourn' chile."

9

*Portia fixed Roman's plate looking frustrated, and had no
idea that Roman had his eyes on another woman at the plantation.
This new girl came to their home after Master Aiken's, wife's sister
moved in with them. Roman had grown tired of Sallie, even before
this new girl, Tabby arrived. He was tired of her nagging ways,
always nagging him about marrying her, and got others on his back
about it too. He had no intention on marrying Sallie, and now
secretly, Tabby has caught hold of his heart.*

Roman snapped his head forward, eyes wide open as if
something startled him. He looked around and realized that he was
sitting in his car. Feeling dazed, he rubbed his eyes, shook his head
and then while squinting his eyes in wonderment, reflected on the
dream he just had. So vivid and annoying was the thought of him
being a slave— house slave at that. He decided that it was 'just a
dream', and went into the house where Neesha was cooking dinner.

"Hey babe, where you been? I called you but you didn't
answer" she said as she was taking the chicken out of the oven.

"I told you I had a meeting with Pastor Stiles after work."

"Oh yeah that's right. I forgot. How did that go?"

"He didn't really have nothing to say. "

"Really? Then why did he ask to have a meeting with you?"
Neesha asked as she
followed Roman out of the kitchen because she could see he wasn't
interested in discussing it with her.

"Look, I'm going to probably take off work one day next
week to turn in the paperwork for my divorce..."

"I thought you did that already!" Neesha said as she
watched him move around their bedroom, hanging his clothes up
that he had brought in with him.

Roman didn't bother to answer her, but continued to hang
his clothes in the closet and then started changing his clothes to get
comfortable before dinner as was his usual routine after work.
Neesha stood there looking at him for a while, realizing that he had
no intention on answering her. She turned and left the room shaking
her head. Roman felt some relief after she walked out because he

10

felt himself getting angry by her questioning. He was on the verge
of telling her to get out of his face and leave him alone, but she left
before he got to that point.

"Roman, dinner is ready if you want to eat. I'm leaving for
choir rehearsal" and out the door she went. She was annoyed with
Roman and the way he kept so closed off to her. She believes he
loves her, but she was shocked that he had not filed for divorce yet.
Rumors are all over the church about them, and she is worried that
she could be asked to 'step down' from participating in the choir for
being involved with a married man, whose wife is also a member of
their church.

*How did I let myself get into this predicament? Everyone
can see that she wasn't right for him anyway, so they shouldn't
blame me. He came after me! I didn't go after him... They've been
separated for months. The divorce is just a formality...* Neesha's
mind was racing as she drove to church. The car seemed to be on
auto-pilot as she pulled into the parking lot and parked because she
was so deep in her thoughts she didn't remember driving there.

Meanwhile, Roman fixed his plate and sat down at the
table to eat. He couldn't seem to get Pastor Stiles' words out of
his head. Although he had no desire to return to Ethel, he began to
wonder how he ended up living with Neesha. Just as he put his
first forkful of food in his mouth, did his phone ring.

"Hello son! How ya doin?"

"Hi Dad. I'm fine... What's going on?"

"Oh nothing much... I just called to see how you're doing. I
haven't heard from you in a couple of weeks. "

"I'm doing fine Dad. I've been meaning to stop by to see you
but I've been real busy..."

"Uh... I got a call from your wife— Ethel called me a
couple days ago. Son, your wife still loves you and she wants
you to go back to your home..."

"I can't believe she called you!" Roman shouted.

11

"Look Dad, I'm done with her and there ain't nothing for us to talk about. I'm getting married soon as I get divorced from Ethel".

Silence.

"Hello? You still there Dad?"

"Yeah, I'm still here" he said solemnly.

"Son, I was really hoping you'd be able to settle down. I guess I haven't been a real good example in your life. Your mother and I struggled in our relationship once she learned that I had been married before I married her. I should have been honest with her about it, but my first wife had run out on me and I had no idea whether she was dead or alive as years went on... still don't..."

"It has nothing to do with you Dad. I made a mistake marrying Ethel. She already had a teenage son and I tried to be a father to him but she wouldn't let me... and I ain't living with no grown teenager who doesn't respect his parents. She yells at me and nagging me like I'm her son. I'm done with that. And it has nothing to do with you or how I was raised. "

"OK son, I'm going to continue to pray for you. I hope you wait and think before you go and marry that woman you're staying with... at least wait for a while..."

"You sound just like Pastor Stiles."

"Well if he told you to wait, he told you right! I have to go, but I will talk to you soon."

Roman hung up the phone and while eating, his mother's voice crept into his thoughts... *Don't be so hard-headed Roman*" he heard her say.

Roman finished eating his dinner and then went into the living room and reclined in his chair to watch TV for a while. He was bothered and perplexed by all that had transpired in this one evening.

"I'm Roman the third, my father is Roman the second. What was that dream about? I wonder how far back our lineage

12

goes with Romans in our bloodline. Am I living out some kind of generational curse?"

Agitated, he got up to get his laptop and decided to start poking around Ancestry.com to continue searching for information about his family, most specifically, his father's side. He had questioned his father from time to time about his family, but his father would become irritated and tell him there was no good reason to be digging up old ghosts of the past. His father's reaction only fueled Roman's curiosity and he became even more motivated to learn about his family's past. He was just jotting down a few names he planned to explore further from a census record he found when the door opened.

"Hi babe" Neesha said as she hung up her coat and walked through the kitchen seeing Roman's plate still on the table. "You finished eating?"

"Yeah."

"Well you could have washed the dishes— there's only a few. I thought we agreed that nights when I have to go out, you will clean the kitchen."

"I never agreed to that."

Neesha just looked at him as he continued to focus on his computer. Roman didn't even bother to look up at her when she spoke. She turned and walked back into the kitchen to clean up, deciding that it wasn't a good time to push the issue. Then, she went into their bedroom and decided to watch TV, and after a while, she decided she wanted to snuggle up with Roman and clear the air. It had felt a little tense in the apartment ever since he came home. She slipped on a sexy nighty, and walked into the living room to get him, only to find him sleep in his chair with the laptop still on his lap. She quietly walked up behind him, and looked over his shoulder to see what was on the screen, but it was dark, in sleep mode already. She glanced down at his notes and saw a few names, some female and she wondered what that was about. Then, she noticed his cell phone sitting next to the note, and she wanted to pick it up, but thought about the fact that he probably had it pass code protected.

"HEY! What are you doing!" Roman suddenly woke up startled and almost knocked his laptop onto the floor.

"Nothing! I was coming to get you so you can come to bed..." and she swept her hands down over his shoulders, but he leaned forward and got up.

Roman looked at her in her sexy nighty, and forgot what he had been doing. He followed her into the bedroom, as if in a trance. She pulled him close, kissing him as she helped him slide out of his clothes, and they fell into a wild ride of phenomenal love-making ecstasy.

When Roman came to, it was morning, but earlier than he needed to get up for work. He laid there for a few minutes, thinking— thinking about what he was doing with his life. He was angry that Pastor Stiles' words had somehow penetrated his mind because he kept thinking about what he said. He looked over at Neesha and wondered why he was with her. Then he started thinking that he needed to get those divorce papers signed, and return them to his lawyer. He planned to do it during his lunchtime that day. Neesha stirred, still sleep, and Roman continued to lay there thinking about how he ended up where he is.

That dream— what could it mean? And who is that woman on the census? Why is she listed as my grandfather's wife? That isn't my grandma's name.

Roman finally got up and decided to shower, get dressed and head to work.

Still in his head, he began to hear Pastor Stiles' words again... '*take your mind off of this obsession to be in a relationship. Do some self-reflection...*'. Roman drove along and asked himself, "*Do I even love her? This is crazy. It's all about sex. I can't think of any other good reason that I hooked up with her. She can't cook...*" and a horn from the car behind him honked, snapping Roman out of his trance at the light. He quickly pulled off, feeling bewildered about himself— irritated that he couldn't think of any good reason he was with Neesha.

"She looks good. She has a job... I wonder if she has her driver's license... Ethel didn't tell me she was driving on a suspended license until the day after we were married. Can't believe I didn't know that. Hmmm. I

14

really don't know much about Neesha, and here we are, walking around saying we're engaged. "

Roman didn't even care if people saw him talking to himself at this point as he pulled into the parking lot at his job. He figured that folks would think he was talking on his cell phone anyway and chuckled at that thought.

Lunchtime, Roman went to see his lawyer as he had planned with all the paperwork signed, and the balance of the fee so that the divorce process can move forward. He walked out of the lawyer's office smiling, feeling a sense of relief that closure was near. He decided to take a stroll through the adjacent park and get a hotdog from the truck that is always parked on the other side. While in line, he felt a tap on his shoulder.

"Hey brother Roman! How you doing?"

"Bernard! How you doing man?"

"I'm good! What you doing out here? I thought you worked cross town?"

"Oh I had some business to take care of. How you like being a deacon?"

"It's good! It's good. So uh, Roman... It's funny I run into you today. We was just talking about you last night."

"Oh man y'all ain't got nothing better to do than to be all up in my business?"

"Naw man, come on. You the one that got your business out there. What could you possible expect, by having a wife and a girlfriend all up in the same church."

"But you know I haven't been with my wife for a long time now. I just finished filing the divorce papers just now! So you can run back and tell that!"

"I'm talking to you as a friend, man. I can understand that you and Ethel are finished. But both you and Neesha... still married, and walking around talking about being engaged..."

"Hold up. What did you just say? What do you mean, me AND Neesha both married..."

15

"Yeah bruh. I had a feeling you didn't know. Not many folks do, because she left him years ago, and he ain't never been the church going type. I know because her husband is my wife's cousin. I have never said anything to her or anyone else. She doesn't know that he and my wife are related or know each other."

Stunned, Roman stepped out of line before ordering his hotdog, and stood there looking at Deacon Bernard with his mouth open.

Roman went back to work and tried to focus on his tasks, but struggled with the anger that has swelled up in his spirit.

"She got a real damn nerve pushing me to get divorced. I can't believe she lied to me like that. I need to drop-kick her ass to the curb" he mumbled.

He grabbed his forehead with both hands and it weighed his elbows down onto his desk. The rollercoaster ride of emotions of the day had given him a headache.

"What am I doing? What am I doing? " He raised his head to look at the clock and saw that it was almost time to leave, so he decided to leave a few minutes early knowing it wouldn't be a problem, and he wasn't able to focus on his work anyway. He began putting his work away and thought about calling Neesha, but decided not to. Pastor Stiles' voice crept into his head— *"You need a period to regroup, to settle down with yourself. Start focusing on God and pray. Get involved in some ministries and take your mind off of this obsession to be in a relationship. Do some self-reflection..."*.

Roman sat down in his car and put the key in the ignition, but didn't turn it on. He kept hearing those words— *"...do some self-reflection..."*. Putting his head back, he tried to remember the last time he was not in a relationship. He couldn't remember being alone since high school, always having a girlfriend, and if she wasn't working out, he'd have another one waiting in the wings.

"What is it? Am I afraid to be by myself? I'm not a sex addict... but seems I just need to know that I can get it when I want it... need a woman at my disposal. Wow... that sounds so cold... not

16

just 'a woman', but a woman who is mine. But how has this attitude served me? What have I gained? It's not fair to them either".

Roman surprised himself by saying that, as if he had never even considered the feelings of his women before, that way.

"And that dream..." Roman said to himself as he turned the car on. He drove out the parking lot with a destination in mind... his father's house.

"He's going to explain this to me. I want to know who that woman is on Grandpa's census record" he said as sped onto the highway.

"Hello son! This is a surprise! What brings you over this way today?"

"Hi Dad. I've been doing some thinking..."

"Uh oh. That's dangerous" his father laughed.

"Alright alright.... All jokes aside, I've really been thinking about what you said, and my meeting with Pastor Stiles". Roman walked into the living room and sat down.

"You want something to drink son? I just made myself some tea."

"No thanks" and he got up to follow his father into the kitchen.

"Dad, I have done some research on our family. Who is Sallie Mae?"

"Who? Sallie Mae? I don't remember no Sallie Mae."

"She's listed on the census record as Grandpa's wife. It shows that Grandpa was around 19 years old..."

"No that can't be right..."

"I believe it is right... you wouldn't know because he didn't marry Grandma until 10 years later. I wonder what happened to this first wife that it seems none of us know about..."

"Just hold on now son. Those old census records..."

"Dad just think about it. It is very possible that you just don't know about this. I wish Uncle Greg was still alive. I bet he might have known since he was older than you. It doesn't show that they had any children."

Roman's father poured the hot water from the kettle over the teabag in his cup and took in the steamy aroma of the herbs, and then sat down and let out a sigh.

"Son, maybe it is true, but why you going on about it? It's old news... there ain't no good reason to go digging up old bones..."

"That's what you older folks are used to but now folks want to know more about their roots. Aren't you even curious about having maybe another line of relatives out there?"

"No... not really" his father said as he sipped his tea.

Roman shook his head and went on talking about it.

"That dream I had was crazy. I'm thinking that as far back as our slave roots, the men in our family have not regarded women right. Selfish maybe. Maybe we were forced to be selfish that way. I don't know. But even you Dad! You had a wife before Mom, and you probably would have never told her if she hadn't heard about it after your hometown cousin visited us. I bet you were going to take that bit of news to your grave..."

"Now son, I have apologized about that over and over again. To this very day I don't know what happened to her. She left me! I had no idea what happened to her."

"So you just act like it never happened, move away and get married to someone else?"

"They say after seven years a person is considered dead..."

"You're supposed to get that legalized though... but that's beside the point. Grandpa did the same thing. That's what gets me. And without even knowing all this, I was about to do the same thing!" Roman stood up and paced the floor as his father watched him.

"And I think that dream was an omen, a sign. It's time for someone to break this chain— this ugly legacy. Dad, I am not trying to make you feel bad. But I'm realizing that we have a common thread I in our lineage and it needs to stop. I think you know that, because you called me and even said it."

Roman's father looked at him but said nothing as Roman sat back down. They continued to talk a little more and Roman assured his father that he meant no disrespect, and was not trying to make him feel bad.

"Well, I know what I need to do, and I believe it was divine intervention that has provided me the opportunity to do it. "

Roman drove home, feeling good about his visit with his father and the conclusion he had come to. But once he parked his

18

car at Neesha's house, his mood immediately changed. He became defensive and geared up for a fight because he planned to tell her that he wants to break up with her. He felt fortunate to have found out about her being married, because it was a perfect excuse for him to use, to get out of the relationship. Still the whole idea of what he was about to do made him feel tense, and he sat in the car for a few minutes to get his words together.

When he entered the house, Neesha was sitting in the living room watching TV. Roman looked around the kitchen and saw no evidence of anything cooking.

"You ate dinner already?"

"I had a sandwich. We're out of bread though. Why don't you run to the store, and then stop by Burger King. I have a couple of coupons..."

"Never mind, I'm not hungry. We need to talk." Roman walked into the living room and sat down.

Silence.

Neesha was sitting there looking at him, intently waiting to hear what he wanted to say, yet he said nothing.

"What is it you want to talk about Roman?"

"I'm moving out. I've thought long and hard about our relationship, and... It's not right. We should have never even gotten together the way we did..."

"WHAT! What are you talking about Roman! What did I do to make you want to leave me?" She got up and went over to the couch where he was sitting and tried to sit in his lap, but he got up.

"Our relationship is wrong, and you know it Neesha. I'm still getting divorced, but what about you!"

She looked at him stunned. "Uh... who told you?"

"It doesn't matter. You have a lot of nerve though, I'll give you that. Pushing me to get a divorce while you're still married. Now that's a lot of nerve" he said as he walked into the bedroom to start packing his clothes.

"Roman! Wait! I was going to tell you. I plan to get a divorce too. I haven't seen him in so long... I needed some money to get the divorce started. I figured once you got yours, you could help me get mine..."

"You must be crazy! I don't want to hear no more about it. You're still married, and separated for more than eight years and

19

you're waiting for me to get a divorce? You should have been done that long before I met you. I've made up my mind. I need some time on my own and I ain't helping you get no divorce. I'm outta here! "

"But what about you and Ethel?"

"I'm getting my divorce. I'm cleaning house. I'm done. You know it's not right Neesha. Our relationship was built on a foundation of sex and I'm finally forcing myself to think higher than that. We have nothing in common really. Have you thought about that? You're a lot like Ethel really, and that's clearly a problem... a problem with me. "

Roman left and then realized that he didn't want to go to his home where Ethel was either. He went back to his father's house and asked if could sleep on his couch for that night while he figured out what his next step would be. The next day, he got up and went to work, and after work, headed to his house where his wife and her son still lived.

Ugh! I guess I'll make my office my bedroom for the time being. I think I'll join the choir or volunteer at the church so I don't have to be home so much. Yeah. That's a good idea. God! Please forgive me! I'm going to fall on my knees when I get home and pray for wisdom and strength. I WILL break this curse. I'm not going to be like the men in my past family line. I'm going to do better and be a better example going forward."

Roman parked, and didn't notice that Ethel's car wasn't there. He felt empowered after praying while driving and decided to let her know that he's moving back in and they can discuss how the divorce should work. He walked in and saw no one. But it was strange and it didn't hit him as to why at first. Then as if by slow motion, his vision began to recognize an empty home. There was nothing on the counters in the kitchen. He opened the refrigerator and saw very little food in there. He went to the living room and saw there was no TV, the recliner couch, gone. Pictures were missing from the wall. He ran to the bedroom and found that pictures were missing but the furniture was still there. He opened her dresser drawer and it was empty. He snatched the closet door open, and her clothes were gone. He ran to her son's room... it was empty.

Stunned, he went into the kitchen and sat down at the table, shocked. Then he saw the note. *"Roman, I'll call to give you an address where you can send the divorce papers. I will sign them. I've decided it is time to move on. Have a nice life because I intend to."*

Roman went into the living room and sat in the one chair that was left behind, put his head back, and closed his eyes. Then he remembered that he had planned to get on his knees, so he did.

"Dear Lord, I thank you and praise you for leading me through this week in ways that are mysterious and miraculous. I thank you Lord for allowing me to hear the wisdom of Pastor Stiles and my father, and that I heard what they said and understood finally how important it is to learn about myself, my goals, my desires. Help me Lord to be accountable and give me peace and patience as I make the effort to reflect on my past in order to have a better future. I thank you, and I praise you Lord, in Jesus name. Amen."

Roman got up and looked around his empty home and started imagining for the first time that living by himself might not be a bad thing at all. He sat down and really felt the weight of Pastor Stiles' words on him in his quiet home. It was a new feeling and experience, and he decided he is ready for the challenge.

Struck by Lightning

2

George stood up during devotions at Sunday morning service and requested prayers from the congregation: "Please pray that my wife gets a better job."

Out of work again after getting hurt on the job, George, clinging to his convalescence months after the incident, stood unashamed. His wife, Sheila, had complained that they needed more money, so he had been inspired to stand that morning. George had never grown up. He had found a woman to play "momma," someone whom he could hang onto like an anchor in a swamp. Working for a living was a foreign concept to him. His goal was survival, and he believed that a woman was required for that endeavor. What a disservice his mother had done to him when she allowed the environment that had facilitated his development into such a dysfunctional man.

Although his father was never around, George's mother did not help matters at all by ignoring his upbringing. George's will to survive had given him some skills though. He had become an expert at sniffing out women with low self-esteem— he was like a hound dog. And once he had made a connection, he knew how to latch on, like a virus to its host.

George's mother had been the host in their parasitic relationship for many years, but she had finally tired of him after many, many infractions, including the incident which had turned out to be the last straw. He had drilled a hole through her kitchen ceiling in order to bring the cable wire from the second floor to the TV on the counter. The wire hung directly in front of one of the cabinet doors, and the wire had to be moved out of the way to open or close the cabinet doors. George's mother had come home from work to find him sitting in the kitchen, waiting for her as usual. Every now and then, if there was food and when he wasn't out pretending to be looking for work, he would cook something.

She hadn't even noticed the wire hanging from the ceiling until she went for a glass and tried opened the cabinet door, only to find it obstructed by the wire. She looked at the TV, then the wire, then slowly followed the wire up until she saw the hole in the ceiling.

"What the hell did you do? Are you crazy, nigga? How you gonna drill a hole in the ceiling, you ignorant black fool! This is not my house!"

She was furious and outdone. She was very frustrated with him for screwing up her life and her home. She hated him, but she knew that it was wrong to feel that way. She experienced guilt every time she had those thoughts, which had become more often over the years. She hated him because he was a reminder of her failures in life. She felt like a failure because her son was useless. Finally, she was done.

Meanwhile, George sat there looking perplexed because he thought she would have been happy to have cable on the kitchen TV. She couldn't decide whether he was clueless and hadn't known it was wrong, or whether he just didn't care and was so damn lazy that he had decided to simply drill the hole in the ceiling instead of going through the trouble to do it right.

"You have to go! And I mean now! No...I'll give you until tomorrow to get your things and get out of here. I've had it! You better get to a shelter or somewhere! I don't care where you go!"

He was completely stunned, and then he got mad. He started yelling at her, saying that he "ain't goin' nowhere," and she, in turn, told him she would call the police. He hated to leave the security of his mother's house, but his survival instincts kicked in, and he realized his next move would be to move in with the woman he had been seeing because she had an apartment. He had not approached her about moving in yet, but this situation has forced him to realize that this was the time to make his move.

It wasn't as hard as he had thought it would be to convince Sheila to let him move in, especially after he had told her he wanted to get married. He told her that they should join a new church and that he wanted to have a family with her. Being that she was divorced and felt lonely and was undeniably desperate, she was thrilled at the attention she was getting from him. Most of the time, she even accepted just about all of his excuses for being unemployed. She rationalized his sporadic work history and trusted him because when he did find work, he brought her money and the occasional, nominal gift. She couldn't wait to go to work and tell the girls in the office that she was getting married.

George presented himself as a "handy man" or a "home improvement man." He had learned somewhere down the line that when people were desperate or trying to get a job done cheap, he had a chance to make some money. He had learned how to sniff these kinds of people out too. Once he knew he had someone's interest, he was really good at convincing them that he could do whatever job they wanted done, mostly because he had convinced himself that he was a jack-of-all-trades.

So George moved in with Sheila, and they got married a few weeks later. During that time, he had found odd jobs here and there and brought the money to her, and she was happy, but in a sad way. It was never much, but the contribution helped her keep their household going. She had a daughter from a previous marriage living with them, and she was getting $50 per month in child support, but it barely paid for her daughter's clothing.

Months and then years passed, and Sheila had become frustrated many, many times with George's sporadic work habits. He kept causing problems in their home by frivolously spending money which they didn't have to spare. She had given him a cell phone, but she had to take it from him because he kept running up the bill and then couldn't pay it. He went weeks without work—sometimes months. He used up all the gas in her car, all the while claiming to look for work. She was falling behind on the rent again.

Her complaints led him to clean up the apartment and to have dinner ready for her when she got home from work. This usually worked for him, and she would immediately get off his back. But one particular time, it didn't work. George had been out of work for over three months and she had had it.

"I want you out of here" she said plainly. "I'm sick and tired of you lying around this house and stalking me at work."

"Where am I supposed to go?"

"I don't care, but you're getting out of here."

George ended up sleeping in the basement of their church's minister's house. But then he made the minister's wife mad. One day

24

while they were out, he decided to tamper with one of their air conditioners, which caused it to fall out of the window and to smash onto the ground. He ended up sleeping in the minister's truck in the Wal-Mart parking lot.

After some professional begging on George's part, Sheila— after a little over a week—finally allowed him to come back into the apartment. That night, he slithered into her bed.

"Let's have another baby," he breathed into her ear through his overly wet lips, which slathered against his toothless gums in the upper front of his mouth.

Over the years, he had truly let himself go. For some reason, she had not noticed until this night, when he had had the audacity to suggest that they have a baby when he couldn't even keep a job.

For an instant, she wondered how she could have even allowed Godzilla to make love to her, and this thought sunk her into a feeling of insanity. She was disgusted with herself for allowing this gargoyle in her bed again after he had slept in the minister's truck the night before. She tried to imagine why she had ever agreed to marry him. His comment about having another baby had pushed her right over the edge and into delusion; she decided to take his comment as a compliment, and she tried to feel good about it.

She kissed his forehead and then turned away from him, which caused him to roll toward her. She felt his huge beer belly on her back before his arms managed to reach over her shoulders. She was lying there and decided to try and enjoy the fact that she could have sex when she wanted it. She thought about how many other women she knew who didn't even have husbands, and they didn't get to have sex whenever they wanted to, at least not like she could. She decided that she was fortunate to be able to have a husband, even if he wasn't working right now. The Bible says for better or for worse she thought.

But right then, it was just like back then, when he was unemployed. He was out of work way more of the year than he was employed. And when he did find work, it was chancy whether he would even get paid because although he marketed himself as a jack-of-all-trades, he was clearly a master of none.

Sheila just recently learned that George was illiterate, and she couldn't believe he had hidden it from her for so long. How could she have missed it? They have been married for eight years now, and

25

she was just now realizing that he couldn't read. But it all made sense when she thought about it. "No wonder he has such a hard time getting a job," she lamented. This had all come out when he had cried on her shoulder after sleeping in their minister's broken down truck in Wal-Mart's parking lot. He had told her that he was having a hard time getting anywhere in life because of his mother. It is all her fault he said, because she didn't care whether he went to school or not, and she had never helped him learn how to read or do anything else. He had told his wife that his mother used to leave him home alone a lot and that she would go out, and when she came back, she would yell at him.

He hadn't mentioned that his mother had worked two jobs, and that one was a third-shift job so she could be home in the morning to get him off to school, and that the other was on weekends at a local bar as a barmaid. She would be so tired in the mornings that she would just get him up and sometimes send him out the door and to school with a 'butter and jelly sandwich. But she never followed up with him from there regarding homework or anything else. Sometimes he went to school, sometimes he didn't.

He was fifty-six years old, but his wife didn't know that either. He had lied when they met when he told her he was only ten years older than her. At the time, she was twenty-seven. In reality, he was sixteen years older than her, but his predatory instincts kicked in, and upon meeting her, he didn't want to take a chance by saying that he was forty-three. He figured that saying he was thirty-seven would sound more palatable. He had gotten tripped up on this lie a couple of times, which had confused her, but she always wrote it off as him having too much on his mind. She actually felt sympathy for him after he had cried about his mother neglecting him, and she decided to use this as an excuse to take care of him. But it had become increasingly harder to do as he bungled his way through life as a grown man with an imbecilic brain that she continued to make an effort to ignore or compensate for.

She had already lost an apartment because he had lied so many times about the jobs he had and the money he was going to make. Time and time again, she allowed herself to believe that he would have the rent money, and time and time again, he came up short or with nothing at all.

Once he took a job with a hazmat company as a trainee, and they explained to him that during the three-week training period, he would make $8 per hour. After that, he would get a certificate, and his salary would be raised to $10 per hour. George was so happy to tell Sheila this. He went to work the first week and struggled because he could not read. However, the workers were showing and helping him get along, but he was the type of man who somehow felt he knew better about things he knew nothing about. So he gave them a hard time by not following instructions, and this caused them to have to do some of the tasks over again.

At the end of the first week, they gave him his check, and he was furious. He had forgotten about the training period and had expected the $10 per hour pay. He went and complained to the foreman, who tried to explain that it was his first week and that he doesn't make $10 per hour yet. He felt that he was being lied to by the foreman and started yelling at the man. He finally told the foreman that he quit.

He was so clueless that he went to another worksite, where the same company was contracted to do some construction, and asked about getting hired there. He had no idea that it was the same company at a different location. The man he was talking to typed George's name into the computer and his record popped up. He called the foreman at the other location and after talking to him, decided that George was mentally challenged, and he told him to go home.

George went home and complained to Sheila that the foreman would not pay him what he was supposed to get. Sheila called his foreman, and he told her what had happened. He also told her that her husband, because he had failed to complete the course, owed the company money for the training materials he had received. She was outdone! She could not believe that her husband went on a job for a week as a trainee, quit, and ended up owing the company money in the end.

After she allowed him back into the apartment and after he no longer had to sleep at Wal-Mart, he had claimed that he was going to find steady work again. As usual, he found day jobs and work through the church members, but not without issues. It was rare that anyone was completely satisfied with his work, and he never accepted criticism as something he could learn from.

27

Whenever anyone complained, he felt attacked and became completely obstinate.

They were already on their third church membership; he had burned many bridges at the other two by getting hired by people in the church and then doing shoddy work. He had disgusted the entire congregation of the second church when he had ended up on disability after one of the deacons had found him a job. Two weeks after getting hired, George claimed that he had hurt his back lifting some wood. He demanded an ambulance and was taken to the emergency room. Based on his complaints, they told him he had a sprain and that a follow up with a doctor would probably allow him disability. He was very happy to tell his wife that. He was happy to tell the church this also. Because Sheila had complained about how tight their money was, the last Sunday when they attended that church, he decided to stand up during testimonials to ask the church to pray that his wife would find a better job.

Sheila had sat there horrified and paralyzed with embarrassment as he stood up and announced to the church that he was unemployed and going on disability, as if he were proud of this accomplishment. She could not hide her stupidity there anymore, and she knew she could no longer attend that church. Even the men in the church were mad at her husband that day, and one of the deacons told him that he should be ashamed of himself for playing games. He clung to the disability story long after being out of work, and the fact was, he was never able to collect any money because he hadn't been on the job long enough. She claimed she was going to sue for a while, but everyone she told that story to knew she was beating a dead horse.

Well, the camel's back broke again—just like it had with his mother—when he claimed he could remodel someone's bathroom by putting tile down and fitting a bathtub in. George had bitten off way more than he could chew, and it wasn't the first time, nor would it be the last. He got this job from some people he had met at the new church they had joined a few weeks after his testimonial at the previous church.

The tile was crooked and didn't meet any of the walls evenly. Some tiles were raised so that the floor had a lumpy effect. The bathtub had been lined with thick spackle and looked very messy. Once the people who had hired him saw the job he had done, they

28

were furious! They wouldn't pay him the second half of the money that he felt he was owed for the job.

He went home to complain to Sheila about the people who refused to pay him the rest of the money they owed him for the job. She called them, like she had done so many times for other mishaps he had done, and asked them what the problem was. After they told her about how horrible his work was, she asked her husband about it, and he said that the reason the floor tiles were uneven was because the house was crooked. She knew right then that this was yet another job he had claimed he could do that was over his head. She knew he would never take responsibility for it, nor would he feel accountable. She tried to argue with the people, knowing she sounded stupid by saying that their house was crooked and that it wasn't his fault. The argument went nowhere, and she gave up.

Sheila buried her head in her hands, wanting to cry. She needed that money to help pay the rent and bills for the month. At that point, they were behind on the gas and electric bills. The landline phone had been cut off for months, but she still had her prepaid cell phone. The rent was overdue, and now she would come up short again because of the late fees.

"I've had enough! You have to leave here! I cannot support you and our kids!" He began to cry, sobbing like a wounded child. And once again, she gave in and just left him sitting on the couch while she went in her room and slammed the door shut. He knew better than to follow her in there at that moment. So he lay down on the couch, and after about twenty minutes, he crept to the bedroom door and knocked lightly. She didn't answer, so he opened it, and she was sitting on her bed still looking very angry. He asked her if he could have a blanket.

"You know where they are!" she snapped.

He closed the door and went to get a blanket from the linen closet, then lay down on the couch and drifted off to sleep. The next morning, he got up and fixed scrambled eggs for breakfast.

"I would have made toast, but we don't have no bread," he told her as she came into the kitchen. She just looked at him and turned around to go and get their daughters up for school and daycare. The school-age daughter came down, looked at the eggs, and said she didn't want any. Sheila sat down and ate in silence. He sat down with her, and after about five minutes, he said that he had

29

another job interview. He asked her if he could take her to work and the kids to school so that he could go on the interview.

Now she really did not want to give him her car again. Last time she had done that, he had used up all her gas and had come up with no results every day for two weeks until the car broke down. But she decided to give him yet another chance to be a man, get a job, and be worth something. She hated her reality and wanted him to prove the world and her wrong. She was tired of covering for him and making excuses for him. She decided that she had better give him her car so that he wouldn't hang around her job all day, showing all her co-workers what a loser he was. He didn't even have the sense to realize how embarrassing it was, which she found incredible.

So they all left the apartment together: He dropped their daughter off at school and the baby at daycare. Then he took her to work, and off he went to some job prospect. A few hours later, he called her and was very happy to tell her that he had been hired to work for a furniture moving company. George was very excited, and he told her that he started the next day. That night, Sheila told him that she would drop him off there in the morning because she needed her car. He agreed because she had caught him off guard, and he hadn't thought of an excuse to take the car to work. But then he realized he didn't need her car when he found out that he would be driving a van to the different worksites to deliver the furniture.

Every day, he made a detour from his route of delivery to go to her office to check on her, which got on her nerves. Sheila kept telling him he was going to get fired if he kept taking those long lunches and breaks. He ignorantly disregarded her warnings. When he wasn't hanging around her office, he was calling her three to four times a day on the cell phone they had given him.

This went on for about two weeks, and once payday came, they told him that they couldn't pay him because the bill for the cell phone, which they had given him to use on the job, was higher than his weekly pay. They had told him from the beginning that he was only supposed to use the cell phone to call the office once he had arrived at his delivery destination and then again when he was leaving.

"What! What you mean I ain't gittin paid! You better git me my money!" he had barked, but the foreman just looked at him with no regard or fear.

He told George that he would front him one hundred dollars, but he was in the hole for over $750 and he was only making five hundred dollars per week. He then showed George the bill, then told him he could have it because it was a copy. George had stomped out of the office and was still stomping when he arrived at the car where Sheila was waiting to pick him up.

"What's wrong?" she asked before he had even closed the car door.

He explained to her that they had refused to pay him and that they were wrong because he claimed that they never told him he couldn't use their cell phone. Sheila was stunned into silence. She turned the ignition on in the car and began to drive in silence. She parked the car, and they all got out. He began to follow her into the apartment, and she turned around and asked him where he was going.

Now, he was stunned. He began to sob about how unfair it was and how they were wrong to charge him without telling him he had to pay for any calls he had made. As she walked through the door, he almost tiptoed in right behind her. She snatched the mail out of the box on her way in. There was a final notice of eviction. In a nearly robotic motion, she got on the phone to a storage company, and then she called a shelter, which she had already inquired about when she had realized that on her own salary alone, she couldn't make it where they were living anymore. She could not support her husband's stupidity anymore.

Sheila told George that he had until the end of the week to find somewhere to go, because she was moving into a shelter apartment and he was not allowed there. He hesitantly said okay, and then he asked her if he could use her car. She gave him the keys, as she was just plain tired. He went to the home of one of the deacons of their new church and cried on his shoulder about his misfortunes at finding work and talked about how his wife was so hard on him and wouldn't give him a chance. The deacon felt sorry for him and said that he could sleep in the spare room in his house. George drove back to Sheila's place and told her that the deacon was allowing him to stay at his house. She was too mentally exhausted to care. She

31

gave him a tall kitchen garbage bag to pack his things in and drove him back to the deacon's house that evening.

The next day, George asked the deacon to drop him off at his wife's job instead of where he worked. When she got there, he was standing outside looking pitiful. He told her that he was staying with the deacon of their church, as if she hadn't known that already. Then he said that he wanted them to do marriage counseling. She just looked at him, and before she could walk through the door of her office, he asked her for her car so he could go to work. She was so mad, but she went ahead and gave him the keys.

"Don't you ever do that again! You ask that deacon to drop you off at *your* job, not at *my* job!"

George was feeling really hopeless, and he asked Sheila if she was trying to get rid of him. She wouldn't answer. This left him feeling so insecure that by the time he got to his job and headed off for a delivery, he had called her—using the company's cell phone. Then he called her six more times that day. Once when he arrived to pick her up, he began to beg her for her ex-husband's phone number.

"Let me have his phone number. I need to talk to him. Please!" He was begging her for her former husband's phone number. She could not even believe her ears that he was asking her for it.

"What do you want it for?"

George said that he wanted the number just to talk to him and to ask him what he needed to do better in order to keep her. *Incredible* she thought, but as she was worn down by the discussion, she went ahead and gave it to him—anything to get him out of her car as she was pulling up to the deacon's house.

That night he tossed and turned, trying to figure out how to get back into her good graces. The next day, he did get the deacon to drop him off at his job, but before he went on his first assignment, he drove his job's van to her job to see her. She saw his van pull up, and she quickly went outside to tell him to keep going and that he had no business there with his company van since he had nothing important to tell her. From there, he took the long route in order to ride past his nephew's house, where George saw him with the hood up on his 1992 Riviera. Opportunity knocked like a stick on a hollow coconut. George jumped out of the van and convinced his cousin to let him work on the car the next day. He told his cousin that it would cost

32

him much less if he let him fix the car than if he were to take it to a shop. George convinced his cousin to bring it over in the morning to the deacon's house where he was staying.

He drove the van back to his job and quit. They were mad that they had wasted time on him. As he was walking out of the door, he heard one of them say that they should bill him for the gas he'd wasted that day as well as for the phone bill.

The next morning, George's nephew showed up and parked the car on the street. George told his nephew that he would have it ready later that evening. George was so happy because the night before he had told his wife that he had quit, but had another job fixing his nephew's car. He couldn't tell whether she was happy or not because she hadn't said anything. She just said okay as she dropped him off at the deacon's house.

She drove away thinking that this was good because she knew he could fix cars. She had seen him work on cars before, and although sometimes he couldn't get them to run, at least he could tell the person what was wrong with it. She thought that he might be able to make his way into a garage as an auto mechanic.

The reality was that he had no real knowledge about what he was doing, but he never would have admitted it. So by the afternoon of the day that the nephew had dropped the car off, she drove by to check on George with one of her co-workers during lunch time. The co-worker was astonished to see a blanket lying on the ground in front of the car with what looked like a thousand nuts, pipes, bolts, wires, and various parts on top of it. Her immediate thought was that the car would never move again. Sheila saw the look on her co-worker's face and was instantly annoyed.

"He knows what he's doing, you know! I've seen him take a whole car apart before."

The co-worker said nothing, but was thinking about letting her know that the goal was to put the car back together and to turn it on.

George had a perplexed look on his face, which changed to anger when they drove up to see the spectacle. He looked over at the car and asked her what she was doing there. He told her that he had no time to talk to her and that he'd call her later. She left with an uneasy, angry feeling welling up inside of her, and the fact that she tried to hide it gave her a headache.

33

Later that evening when the nephew showed up, he found his car with the hood up and the guts lying in the street. He was outraged and out of control! He started yelling and screaming so loud at his uncle that the deacon's wife came outside to see what was wrong. And then before she could reach them from her front stairs, she saw his nephew retrieve a bat out of the car he drove up in, and in what seemed like slow motion, she watched him raise it and come down right on his uncle's shoulder. George scrambled to get away, but the nephew caught him again on the leg.

By this time, it seemed most likely that a neighbor called the police because they drove up during the assault and took the nephew away. They called an ambulance and George was taken to the hospital. When Sheila arrived to the emergency room, he began to sob about how the nephew hadn't given him a chance to finish. He said he needed another day, but the nephew wouldn't hear it. She would not admit to herself that she knew that the fact was that he could not have fixed that car in a hundred more days.

Again he was in over his head. And then all of a sudden, in a twist of delusion like a flash of lightning which numbed areas of intellect and intuition shooting through her brain, she saw him as pitiful and decided that he was her man and that no one was giving him a break.

That night, he began to cry and tell her that he had problems because his father was never in his life and that his mother treated him like her slave. He went on and on until both of them were crying. Her mentality was affected by that lightning in her brain which could be diagnosed as a nervous strain, which had enhanced her delusion and allowed her to decide that she had to help him and take care of him. She allowed him back into her bedroom despite the threat of being thrown out of the shelter apartment because she decided that this man loved her so much. She rationalized that all this misfortune was not his fault and that they were married for better or for worse.

And he smiled when he woke up next to her in the morning.

Signs for the Blind

3

"It's not what you think!" he yelled when she appeared at the foot of their bed where he lay with a man she had seen in the neighborhood.

Tonya didn't even feel her mouth drop open as she stood there and tried to reconcile her mind with her eyes. Lewis snapped up in the bed as the other guy was scrambling to get his clothes on. She stood there in shock as he continued to talk. He was talking fast, but it seemed like her ears were shut. Actually, she was hearing words come out of his mouth, but it was like some kind of alien language. She stood there frozen as his mouth continued to move.

Lewis was so relaxed in his arrogance that he wasn't even worried that Tonya might come home and catch him in the act. But come home early that day she did. She had made an excuse to get off work early because she was tired and hung over from the night before. Her supervisor was tired of her coming in late, calling in sick, and now claiming to be sick so she could leave early. Tonya knew that this was not going to sit well with her supervisor, but she was feeling woozy and her head was hurting.

That morning when she drove to work in her car, which was barely running, she wondered why she was still smoking weed. She had already decided that she wasn't drinking that much but had had a little too much the night before, which she figured was usually a sign that she was drinking too much, and then quickly put that thought out of her mind. She had told herself she was getting too old to be hanging like that, but at the end of the day, she always found herself craving a joint and some wine.

Tonya regained consciousness as the door opened and the cold air hit her as the other guy who was in bed with Lewis ran outside. She heard Lewis saying things like "you don't understand… We were just lying here… I was already laying down when he came over… He said he couldn't go home and just laid down…"

She felt like she was in autopilot as she turned toward the closet and grabbed her largest suitcase.

"Hey! Where you going?" she heard him ask as she laid the suitcase down on the floor and opened it.

Tonya never even turned around to see Lewis get up and put his pants on. Horror began to creep into her mind as she thought about laying in that bed night after night, probably on some other man's cum, which had mixed with her man's juice as he and some man splashed all up inside each other.

That thought sent her flying straight into the bathroom, where she promptly threw up, almost making the toilet. Instead, it hit the floor, rug, and ran down the side of the toilet. A little did actually go in the toilet though. She stood up and looked at the mess and the mess on her clothes. She turned to grab some Clorox wipes from under the sink, but the asshole was standing behind her already with the Clorox wipes in his hand.

"Here, let me help you." But Tonya wasn't having it.

"Get the hell away from me" she said in a plain and evenly paced voice.

She snatched the Clorox wipes from him and began to clean up the mess. She wondered why she wasn't crying. She started thinking about how she would never be able to even tell anyone about this. She figured she had to tell her mother because that's where she was headed.

"Nope, I'll just tell her we had a fight, and I am through with him," she decided. The real truth was just too ugly to express.

"Will you please listen! Where are you going? Nothing was happening! We were just lying there..."

"Under the damn covers? Come on! Please!" She wiped her face and changed her clothes, talking to herself out loud about him being a fucking faggot.

"Listen bitch! You ain't takin' nothin' out this house!"

He was furious that he had been busted, but he was even madder that she was packing her things. Tonya continued moving and packing her bag as the thoughts of HIV and AIDS began to sail through her mind like a neon scrolling banner.

"You better git your fuckin' hands off me you nasty ass bastard! I am outta here!"

Lewis had grabbed her arm, trying and make her stop packing and listen to him, but her voice and expression finally let him know it was to no avail to try and reason with her at that moment. He backed off because he started thinking about how many times she had left him, only to come back. And with this thought, he decided to just back away and let her leave so she could have the opportunity to calm down and come to her senses. He knew damn well she wouldn't stay long at her mother's house, where she had been molested by her father as a kid. Her mother resented her for it, too, so he knew that although her mother would allow her to stay there for a little while, it wouldn't be for long.

The other assurance he had was that she didn't make enough money to get a place of her own. And over the years, he had already convinced her that she was lucky he wanted her. He never came right out and said those words, but he had found ways to reinforce it in her mind. He felt in control that way.

She zipped up her suitcase and walked straight out of the door, jumped into her car, and drove toward her mother's house. As she was driving, she began to wonder how she had allowed herself to move back in with him after she had left him so many times before. The last time she left was because he had started busting into the bathroom while her ten-year-old daughter was in the bathtub a little too regularly. Her daughter was downright upset about it. She realized she couldn't leave her daughter alone with him. He wasn't her father after all, and she realized that he was being inappropriate.

But… instead of leaving him right then, she had moved her daughter out, letting her mother keep her. Tonya moved her daughter into the very house that her grandfather, Tonya's father, had molested her when she was a little girl. But her focus had been on herself and her selfish desires, not past horrors, in regard to her own father's proclivity. She had decided that removing her daughter from the apartment where she and her boyfriend lived was her best option. This way she could continue living away from her parents, get high when she felt like it, and have her man there with her. Lewis wasn't even working during this time. He had lost his job a few months prior and was collecting unemployment.

Now she wondered what the hell she had been thinking to do something like that. "It had to be the weed," she thought. "Or maybe I had a nervous breakdown," she pondered. As she tried to think of excuses, she thought about how she hadn't left him for months after removing her daughter from their apartment, not until she had found out he had molested his own daughter when she had spent the night. His daughter was thirteen years old. As it turned out, she learned that it wasn't the first time he had tried that either. The night she had heard his daughter crying in the other bedroom—the room where her daughter used to sleep—she went in to see what was wrong. Lewis's daughter told Tonya that he had come in the room while she was asleep and forced her panties off. She cried uncontrollably as she choked out her words, saying that he had tried to force his "dick" into her, as she called it. She told Tonya that she had struggled so much that he finally gave up. He told her she better not tell anybody or he would "whup" her ass.

Devastated and disgusted beyond belief, she had confronted him and threatened to call the police if he did not arrange to get help. She was feeling especially guilty, but could not admit to herself where that feeling came from, other than from the fact that she had been at the bar that night, picking up some weed. That guilt really stemmed from the buried intelligence she had about this pedophile— this beast. He had been eyeing her daughter, and she had done nothing but allow her own daughter to fall victim to him.

She called his mother, and to her shock, his mother said she wasn't surprised about this because he used to rape his gay brother when they were teenagers. His mother went on to describe how he would catch his younger brother at home alone and throw him down across his bed and rape him, all the while screaming, "You wanna be a faggot? I'll show you what it means to be a faggot!" His mother went on to say that she had gotten counseling for him back then. His mother's denial allowed her to believe it had helped him. The fact that she wasn't surprised showed that she had some buried intelligence too.

As Tonya continued the drive to her mother's house that night, after finding Lewis's heinous ass in bed with that man, she was again wondering at which point in time she'd had the nervous breakdown that allowed her to continue seeing this man. She thought about how he had sought therapy after that incident with his daughter during which she had threatened to call the police. She had moved in with her mother after the incident, where her daughter had already been living in the meantime. But how had she ended up back

38

with him? She could not remember right off how she had managed to find herself back in another apartment with Lewis.

Remarkably, it was about three months after the incident with his daughter that she was back in full swing with Lewis again, as he claimed he had been cured of his twisted ways. He apologized profusely and she believed him. So needy was she to feel wanted that she tucked all of that nightmare away in a far corner of her brain. She was craving the touch of a man, and although in the beginning when she had first moved out she had said she would never speak to him again, she began taking phone calls from him about one week later. All that strong talk in her head about how she was going to hang up on him and how she was going to tell him to never call her again just fizzled when she heard his voice.

Tonya's mother was annoyed as soon as she arrived after that incident happened with his daughter. This was a woman who had become accustomed to being blind about things around her, living in a private, self-imposed prison of her mind. She had somehow chosen many, many years ago to put priority on being married and appearing happy while becoming proficient at rationalizing and justifying the ugliness around her that existed under her own roof. She knew her husband was sick and demented, but she could not allow herself to accept it. She knew that he was being inappropriate with his daughters, but she refused to acknowledge it. All those trips he made during the early morning hours up the stairs to his daughters' room bothered her to the point that she began drinking during the day. No one even knew she was an alcoholic for years because she hid it quite well.

And Tonya's father mentally abused her mother even more because her mother knew he had mistresses on the side. Her mother had learned to not say anything to him about it. The one time her mother asked him about a woman she had heard about from a neighbor, he ranted on so much about her being stupid and worthless that she never brought it up again. The problem was that Tonya's mother actually believed she was deficient because she had never worked and had only an eighth-grade education. She was seventeen when she married this man, and he was twenty-nine. Because she got pregnant, her parents demanded that he marry her, and he did. She acted like she didn't know about the mistresses over the years, but everyone who knew about them knew that she knew, because her children had caught him out with other women many times, and so had other people in the neighborhood, and people talk. She played it off in her mind and decided that she was glad he had someone else to lie with because she did not have any feelings for him like that anyway. Sex for her with him had become a mechanical event where she would just lie there and let him get it over with.

Meanwhile, Tonya and her sisters hated their mother for not protecting them from their father. They loved her though, too, because she was their mother, but they had no respect for her. It was the kind of love/hate relationship that would torment Tonya's mother at every turn. And now she was preparing to watch her daughter Tonya become the same kind of woman she was, which was tearing her apart.

So when Lewis's phone calls began to come, Tonya's mother did not slam the phone down on him to try and help her daughter stay away from him. She was hoping that Tonya was not going to stay in her house long, so she kept telling her that Lewis was on the phone, and letting Tonya decide whether to pick up or not. This went on for about one week. He called every day until Tonya finally decided to speak to him. Her mother knew that once she had spoken to him, she'd move out.

And she did move back into an apartment with him soon after, where she found him in bed with a man. "Damn!" she exclaimed as she pulled into the parking space in front of her parents' house. She sat there in the car for a few minutes and thought about so many things at once she had to close her eyes and lean her head back. She finally collected her thoughts and decided to focus on one thing, and that was to go inside and find the cot she would sleep on in the room with her daughter, and then go to the bar and have a big shot, maybe two or three. She decided she needed a drink, and was hopeful she would find a joint too. She was calculating in her mind how many months she had been there with him before moving into her parents' house again. It had been a little over six months this time. Not long compared to the other times she had gone back to him. *But this is it,* she thought to herself.

Tonya got out of her car and opened the trunk to retrieve her suitcase. By the time she entered the gate and walked up the stairs to the door of the house, her daughter opened it and was very glad to see her. Tonya hugged her daughter and then walked up the stairs to put her suitcase down. She then walked back downstairs to where her mother was in the kitchen putting away the food that they'd had for dinner. Her mother just kept moving around in her usual fashion, going from the stove to pick up a pot, then to the counter where the container she was going to store the leftovers in sat, then to the refrigerator where she stored them. She said nothing, and never even turned around to face Tonya.

"What did you cook for dinner?" Tonya finally asked.

Her mother said without turning, "Do you want something? You can fix a plate and throw it in the microwave—"

"No thanks— I'm really not hungry. I need to stay here for a little while until I find an apartment. I'm done with Lewis! I mean it this time." Tonya sat down at the kitchen table and put her head in her hands.

"I found him in bed with a man".

This news made her mother turn around with the pot in her hand and look up at her daughter. "A man. You mean, a man?"

"Yes Mom, a man! And I cannot go back there."

Her mother spun around and began to wash the dishes. She was only speechless for a few seconds before finding her voice again. Tonya's mother was good at suppressing outrage, as she had had much practice within her own lifetime of madness.

"You know where the cot is," she said, and she continued washing the dishes as Tonya went back up the stairs to get it and make up her bed. She began to wonder if she should have seen signs of his down-low infidelity. Many questions swirled through her mind— *How could I have believed him after knowing he had gay sex with his own brother? How could I have ignored this?*

And even when he had tried to have anal sex with her, it didn't jog her selective memory because her priority was always to have a man. She decided to let him actually try once since he kept insisting, but it hurt so badly she made him stop. And she always felt that it was disgusting anyway.

Tonya realized that she was frowning as she reflected on her relationship with Lewis. She felt that sick feeling come on again as she thought about how, over and over again, she had decided that Lewis was a man who wanted her, and how she felt that since there weren't many men who worked and had valid driver's licenses who

41

were kicking doors down to be with her, he would have to do. But this time, she was convinced that their relationship was over.

As weeks went by, in predictable fashion, Lewis began to call. But this time Tonya did not take his calls. Her mother was very surprised at this, and was almost resentful because her daughter was showing strength that she never had. She started telling Tonya she should talk to him, and their conversations would end up in bitter arguments between them. Tonya just could not get past the visual image that was burned into her brain, of Lewis lying in the bed with that man.

And then one day, after a month had gone by, Tonya was on her way out of the house and Lewis was standing up against her car. She stood frozen on the front porch and then finally yelled over to him, "What are you doing here?"

"I need to talk to you! Why haven't you taken my phone calls?"

She threatened to call the police and he just stood there. She then walked across the street and right past him, opened up her car door, got in, and pulled away, almost knocking him down because he was leaning on the car.

When she came out of work that same day, he was standing in the parking lot, drunk and waiting for her. She told him she was going to file a restraining order against him. Tonya got into her car and as she pulled out of her parking space and headed for the exit of the lot that led onto the highway, she saw him stumble, running behind her car, but she just peeled out into traffic and sped away.

Lewis continued to quickly stagger through the parking lot toward the highway and suddenly, before reaching the exit, he was run down by a car that seemed to come out of nowhere. The car dragged his body about twenty feet before it stopped, backed up and left the parking lot. The car pulled into traffic and sped off. Ironically, no one was close enough to get a good look at the car, which Lewis's brother was driving, or the license plate on it.

That night Tonya got a phone call from Lewis's mother, who told her what had tragically happened to her son. Tonya was numb as she dropped the phone back into its cradle. She became emotionally confused when she heard that he had been violently killed while chasing her as she drove out of that parking lot. She went to sit down on the couch in the living room and felt a tremendous, yet guilty, relief. *It is over,* she said to herself. *I am free.*

Bells and Whistles

3

"I need some money," he came right out and said after deciding he had planted enough bait on the hook of his pseudo romance.

Carol could not believe he had asked her for money and she just looked at him and then chuckled.

"Oh! So that's what this is about!" she said as she laughed cynically.

She didn't even give him a chance to tell her how much money he wanted as she reached into her wallet and threw $20 at him and told him to kiss her ass as she left.

After seeing Jeff in the neighborhood lounge over the course of a couple of years and not even being sure he was all that attractive, Carol somehow managed to attract his attention. Now the entire initial scene was suspect in her mind, because prior to his coming over to her and buying her a drink the first night that he did so, he had completely ignored her.

Carol knew he was in pursuit of a booty call. "But hell, I haven't been involved with a man in a while, so why not" she said to herself. He definitely was not her type, as Jeff was so typically light skinned and shallow in such a stereotypical way. She had just thought it was odd that he had finally decided to speak to her after all that time. She had decided his motive was sex, and she had decided to be down with the idea.

She had been going it alone for a while after her last breakup and wasn't really in search of a relationship. She decided that she wasn't accepting any more anchors, and she felt like a pioneer amongst her peers because many of them could not understand her new attitude. She began to travel alone, and she found out how much she enjoyed the relaxation and freedom in doing that, which reinforced her confidence in being single and happy.

Her mother and aunts were always hounding her about finding a man. And they usually accused Carol of having something wrong with her, such as being too tough or too smart or having standards that were too high. They kept telling her to dumb it down. But that was just ridiculous based on the men she ended up with. She usually made more money than the men she dated, though she wouldn't let on that she did unless she was asked. And then she was usually sorry she revealed it because it somehow always changed the relationship. What really got on her nerves were the comments she kept hearing about joining a church to find a man. "Lord!" she would exclaim every time she even thought about that idea.

The last church Carol was a member of she had left because one of the deacons would not leave her alone. He was married and his wife was pissed off every time Carol attended church or any of the programs, as if it were her fault that he came after her. He would give Carol cards on holidays with his cell phone number in them, and he always found himself near her, smiling like a damn snake. Not only was his wife angry, but the other deaconesses were also angry at Carol, and the vibe was just ugly, so she stopped going there and hadn't really bothered with being a member of any church in a while. She would just visit various churches on occasion.

What helped Carol embark on her solo endeavors was a time she was sitting alone in a restaurant after work during which she observed people as they came in and out and sat all around the place. She noticed there were other single women there who were eating and reading magazines and talking on cell phones. It seemed as if she had just noticed how many women were seemingly in the same situation as she was—a situation which she refused to consider a predicament. And it wasn't a predicament, because the situation she had gotten out of had been a predicament. Her ex-boyfriend had been very difficult to extract from her life. She had made his life so easy that she spoiled him to the point that he decided he didn't even need to work. She accepted him into her life knowing that he made a lot less money than she did, but she had decided that she wouldn't hold that against him as long as he worked. But he struggled with the fact that she was so independent, and so he demonstrated his control issues in other, usually ignorant ways, the worst being that he would act like an ass in front of her friends. Carol realized that she just could not take him to office parties or almost anywhere else where her friends, family, or co-workers would be. He was simply too immature to even try to fit in, and he harbored resentment toward her and her lifestyle, although he would never admit it. The one and only time she brought him to an office party, he got drunk and started talking louder and louder as he drank more and more at the open bar. He started demanding that she fix him a plate and bring him this and that, and he yelled for her from across the room like a little kid when she ventured off to talk to others at the party—it was a real mess.

So here she was in her neighborhood after-work lounge, and she decided that there was no sense in sitting around waiting for Prince Charming. After talking for a little while at the bar in typical 'pick-up' style to this young guy who had never paid attention to her before, the deal was set, and she left with him and followed him in her car to his house. He was so corny and ridiculous to act like they were going there so she could see his jazz collection. But she just wrote this nonsense off as him being young since he was only twenty-nine, and she, forty-one.

Once they got to his house, she went in with him. She was quite impressed that he owned it— so he said. She already knew that he worked for the fire department. In no time at all, it seemed, they tore each other's clothes off, and she couldn't even remember how they got to screwing right on the floor because it happened so quickly.

Damn! Has it been that long? she thought as she got up and got dressed. She laughed to herself because she had never done anything so spontaneous before. It felt liberating. She felt empowered. Jeff kissed and hugged her as she was leaving and she didn't really expect to be with him again.

A few days later, Carol was sitting at her desk at home, and she began talking to herself.

"Another night where I'm alone and feeling too anxious to sit in the house."

She considered it PMS and then decided that she needed some air, and since she was also hungry, she decided to go out to get something to eat.

"Now, what is it I have a taste for? I guess I'll check the newspaper to see if anything jumps out at me."

As she prepared to go out and eat because she didn't feel like staying in, she mumbled to herself out loud. She didn't feel like going back to that bar because she didn't want to give Jeff the impression that she was looking for him.

Carol pulled into the restaurant parking lot, parked, and confidently walked to the door, where the maître d' asked her if she needed a table for two. She had long since moved beyond the embarrassment of saying no to that question, and simply stated that she was alone and needed a table for herself. She was escorted to a table by the window, which she preferred, and scanned the menu. She had promised herself she wouldn't eat the bread, but as soon as they dropped the basket on the table, she automatically reached for it and the butter. "Ummmmmm, it's warm" she said to herself.

After her nice, relaxing dinner in that nice restaurant that she treated herself to every now and then, she felt good. She felt blessed and fortunate that she could afford to do things like this. And she smiled about what she had done a few nights before, because it was so out of character for her, but she found it freeing to have a sexual romp with a guy she had no intentions of having a relationship with.

A few days after that, Carol stopped by the neighborhood lounge, and there he was. After mingling a bit, she sat down at the bar and ordered a drink. Jeff came right over to where she had sat down and told the bartender to put it on his tab. In the back of her mind, she knew that this attention was making her slightly retarded as she lost all logic and decided to go home with him again. So here was the second encounter, and she was now wondering if something was actually going to come of this. At the same time, in the back of her mind, where she tucked her intelligence away, something was nagging her subconscious by whispering that this calculating asshole had a motive. But her frontal lobe took over and spoke louder as she decided to relish in her inflated ego, deciding that this guy just wanted her.

A couple of days after that last encounter, Carol flew to Las Vegas for an extended weekend getaway. She had planned this trip a few months prior and she was just glad to be getting away to the glitz and glamour of the spa treatments she had made some appointments for in the luxury hotel she would be staying in. She boarded the plane, turned toward the window she was sitting next to, and leaned her head on it. As the plane lifted off the runway, she began to think about the young trick of hers that she had left at home.

Telepathy may have been what caused him to suddenly think about her as he sat in the lounge at the bar. He eventually asked, and was told she had flown to Las Vegas. Jeff was somewhat insulted that Carol hadn't mentioned it to him. He had been thinking that the old woman couldn't get enough of him, and here she had the nerve to fly away just like that.

She returned five days later feeling refreshed and alive. She loved her life, and life in general. She had no intentions of allowing anyone to shake her serenity. The next day, after she returned, she stopped in the lounge and was told that her young guy had been looking for her. Carol laughed and said that was nice, and made the effort to not put too much thought into it. She couldn't help but be flattered, though. And in he came, soon after she had gotten there. So they had their third encounter and she gave him her phone number at his request. The fourth time they met, he had actually called her at her home. She was surprised because this now seemed like he was making a move forward in their very casual connection. So they talked a little, and yet she detected a little pushiness in his conversation about getting her over to his house. She really wasn't feeling it that night, but she decided to go anyway. This time they didn't even make it up the stairs to his bedroom and ended up screwing right on the stairs. *Thank God for carpet,* she was thinking as she wondered if she had rug burns on her back.

After she got herself together, she was about to pour herself a glass of wine when he came up to her and, with no finesse whatsoever, told her he needed some money.

Boom! Reality came rushing in like a tsunami. Carol laughed because this actually made her feel like she was right about him all along.

"What a fool you are," she mumbled as she continued to chuckle. He actually thought he was good enough that he could just put that out there this soon and with little effort to snow her over on his part.

"Oh my God," she laughed as she tossed him a $20 bill and headed for the door, still laughing. He was insulted.

"Wait a minute," he yelled as she walked out the door. She never heard from him again, and never saw him in that bar again. It was like he had disappeared from the face of the earth. She chalked it up to yet another experience; one that left her unscathed.

48

"Thank God!"

Raising The Bar

4

"Uhmmmmmhhh" was the raspy moan she heard as she came through the door. She wondered what the hell he was making that sound for.

Marsha worked the midnight shift from twelve to eight, and had gotten home early because someone had given her a ride. Taking the bus would have taken considerably longer in the morning, but one of her co-workers offered because of the impending threat of snow. Craig didn't even hear her unlock the door and open it. So when she stepped into the dining room, she discovered her drunken boyfriend with his penis in her eight-month-old baby girl's mouth.

"Git your fuckin' dick off my baby you sick motherfucker! What the fuck are you doin? What da hell? What is wrong with you, you sick asshole!?"

Craig jumped backward so far that both his feet literally left the floor, and he fell on top of the coffee table, knocking the coffee cups half-filled with tea from days before onto the floor along with his pint of cheap vodka and other clutter. He scrambled up and fell back onto the couch, still saying nothing with his eyes stretched wide open.
She ran over to the table where her baby was sitting in her carrier and snatched her up and ran to the bathroom to wash the baby's mouth out. She was screaming and crying the entire time, which caused the baby to cry.

"I'm gonna kill you motherfucker! You better get out of my house now! I'm gonna cut your dick off you low-life, sick bastard!"

Craig started crying. He was yelling and sobbing from the living room, where he was still lying on the couch, that he was sorry and he was drunk and didn't know what he was doing. He begged her to please believe him. He was yelling from the couch that he had been sleeping and the baby woke up. He said he didn't remember getting the baby and putting her on the table. He was sobbing and could hardly talk because he was coughing and slurring his words. He said that he was sorry he got drunk, and that it wasn't his fault because one of his buddies brought him the vodka. He continued to plead with her, yelling so that she could hear him as she sat down on top of the toilet lid, holding her baby.

Craig's neighborhood friends were alcoholic, unemployed bums too. It seemed like the purpose of their lives was to do odd jobs around the neighborhood so they could muster up enough change to get a pint of something. Some of them looked about twenty years older than they were, but they were all in their mid- to late forties except the young bum who hung around them. He was much younger than the others. He must have been a bum-in-training, as he was still in his twenties. He lived on the couch of his Aunt's house and claimed he was a rap producer. He had a souped-up karaoke machine with a couple of large external speakers attached, and a CD recording deck. He usually spun stories to the older bums as they drank wine together about how he was renting out his studio to some upcoming rap artist—the studio being his aunt's closed-in back porch.

Craig's drinking partners did not always come around him, especially if they knew he had no money or he was in trouble with Marsha. But on this particular night, one of them came to Craig's place, so he claimed, with a fifth of extra-cheap vodka. Soon after, the young bum came to brag to the others that he had a date with a woman who was going to take him out to dinner. They sat around for a little while laughing as the young bum described how he was going to get her to work him over and how he planned to splash his seed all over her face. After the young bum left, the friend who had brought the vodka left and came back with another fifth. This time he only drank almost half, and left the rest.

As Craig sat there on the couch feeling confused and perplexed at his own heinous actions, he began to think it was the fault of the young bum for putting those thoughts of sex in his head while the other bum forced him to drink that cheap vodka. Marsha told Craig that he may as well drink lighter fluid when she saw him with that cheap liquor. She hated his drinking, and she complained about it so much that he usually hid it from her, or so he thought. She always knew about it, and always saw evidence of it when she got home in the mornings. However, those episodes had been infrequent for a while and she would usually come home to find him and the baby asleep. But lately she was finding that he had been drinking more often than not.

She knew how he smelled when he was drinking so well that she realized that her Korean supervisor, whom she called Scratch n' Sniff, was a drunk. She would almost vomit sometimes when Scratch n' Sniff would walk by her desk with that familiar alcoholic odor. She would laugh to herself when she thought about how Scratch n' Sniff got her name from being busted all the time by co-workers who would catch her scratching her crotch and then sniffing her fingers. It amazed and annoyed her that she couldn't get away from that drunken smell even at work.

Marsha was thinking about how insane it was that she had left her baby at home with this fool Craig, knowing that he's an alcoholic. But when she saw that he had slowed down on his drinking after the baby came, she managed to convince herself that it would be safe to leave the baby with him overnight because, most likely, they would be sleep.

While she was out on maternity leave, there had only been a couple of times that he had not made it home and she'd had to retrieve him from where ever he was because he was so drunk he could not walk. She forced him into the VA detox program, telling him that he had to leave if he could not help her by watching the baby when she went back to work. He agreed reluctantly, and went into the program. He was doing well when she went back to work after about three months, but then she began to notice that he would stay out longer in the evenings before she had to get up to go to work. She had smelled alcohol on him a couple of times after she started working, too, and she went berserk when this happened. Then he seemed to straighten up. By this time the baby was almost seven months old. Usually she would have the baby asleep by the time she left, so he really had to do nothing with her.

Marsha was still sitting on the toilet lid, holding the baby, and she was finally settling down. *He's not well and he's out of work*, she lamented to herself. *That's why he was out of his mind,* she decided. She was sitting there thinking about how she would have to sign him back into the VA because he was going to drink himself to death. She decided that he was in a drunken blackout and did not know what he was doing. She hadn't seen him tie one on like this in months.

When the baby finally settled down, she got up and walked out of the bathroom with the baby in her arms. Craig was now lying across the couch, seemingly unconscious. She left him there, twisted up and halfway on the floor, and went to bed. She locked her bedroom door and kept the baby in the room with her. She couldn't sleep because she was wondering how she would be able to afford a babysitter or daycare.

She began to think about how Craig had lost his driver's license and wrecked her car so many times while driving drunk that on the occasions when he decided to steal her car keys, she would immediately call the police. He claimed he would stop doing that, but she knew she could never fully trust him, which was why she never bothered to even retrieve her car from the impound lot. It had been there since the last time he stole it, and the car was totaled. Marsha would sleep with the car keys under her pillow, under her head, but somehow he would manage to get the keys anyway. Craig had hit a guardrail on a curved road and gotten locked up the last time. Marsha decided to live without a car after that happened, which is why she began taking the bus to and from work.

She was trying to imagine how he would make it if she put him out. Whenever she got mad at him, she somehow started thinking about how he loved her, and then she felt sorry for him and believed she had to take care of him, as if he was helpless. She told herself she had to get him into that VA detox program again.

Marsha had decided long ago that she'd never get out of the ghetto she was living in. *But it's not so bad*, she surmised. She thought about how it's a little cluttered, but she kept the roaches down to a minimum and made sure that she, the baby, and Craig had food. It had been tough because he had been out of work for so long. Craig had exhausted his unemployment pay since getting fired from his job at the grocery store. Even though he said that someone else put the shrimp in his bag, she still wondered if he was lying about getting caught stealing that shrimp. However, and as usual, she gave him the benefit of the doubt.

Having the baby was not planned, but she had stopped taking her birth control pills a few months before she got pregnant because she had kicked Craig out. Before the baby came, she couldn't even stand him touching her when he was drunk. They would fight, and he would try to rape her sometimes, but he would be so drunk and had lost so much weight that he could not overpower her. But he would be relentless sometimes, and she would have to leave and stay at a friend's house.

She knew she was through with him after the last time he wrecked her car while driving drunk. After she got him out of jail, she told him he had to leave. She told him she didn't care where he went. He got drunk that night and came back to her apartment, cussing her out, and she had to call the police. She didn't know where he was going, but he ended up staying with his brother, who was no better than him.

She eventually let him come back because he cleaned himself up and got a job. Prior to that, she let him come over once in a while because she felt the strong sexual urge to be held, and she slipped into her fantasy world of love. He managed to ease his way right back into her home and her life, and she wound up pregnant. She still told herself and other people that she didn't know how it happened. She even said that to the doctor at the clinic.

"He's just drunk," she began to reason, and she began to wind her rationality around the fact that he didn't drink all of the time.

"He has to get help now before he ends up like he was before. Other than this night, on which I found him in an insane act with my child, he's been good at watching the baby", she told herself.

Usually, they were both asleep when she left for the factory she worked at. She'd never had any problem like this from him before. He must have been half-asleep and drunk to do something like this. Besides, the baby didn't know what had happened to her, she figured.

A few hours passed when Marsha heard Craig lightly knocking on her bedroom door. She opened it, and he was standing there with tears in his eyes, and she pushed past him and went to the dining room and put the baby into her carrier. As she turned, he grabbed her and tried to kiss her. She tore away from him because his breath was so foul that it turned her stomach.

"Please! Clean yourself up and brush your teeth, and then come and talk to me."

He did as she said and came back to her as she was picking up the mess that was made when he had fallen onto the coffee table. He grabbed her again and began whispering while holding her that he was sorry and that he had been drunk and that he hadn't known what he was doing.

"Please believe me," he said.

"I better not ever catch you doing anything like that again. I will kill you" she shouted.

After a feeble attempt to pull away from him, she gave in and they hugged and kissed.

He began telling her how much he loved her and how he could not live without her. He said he didn't know what he would do if he didn't have her. She was subconsciously disgusted, and it showed on her face for a few seconds, but then she looked at him and felt pity and somehow responsible for him. She told herself that he loved her and he would die without her.

Before she went to work, Craig told her he was going to AA meetings starting that night. She was glad to hear this. And once evening came, he asked her to go with him to the church where the meetings were held. She went in with him, pushing the baby stroller, and she sat in the back while he went up front and found a seat. Marsha was proud of him for his idea to go to a meeting.

They left together and calmly walked home to the apartment. She took a short nap, got up as usual, fed the baby, and then rocked her to sleep. As she left for work that night, she remembered—

Tomorrow's another day.

After the Fact

5

"Uh…You know I'm married…" Charles revealed as they lay there in bed after a hot, steamy sex romp that made her see stars.

Joan laid there trying to reconcile what she had just heard while she also tried to collect her mind after having the best orgasmic release of her life. She wondered as she lay there saying nothing, if she had known all along and had been in denial. She could not believe that she'd had no clue, but then she realized it was because she'd had no intentions of ever getting hooked up with this man at the time he started his pursuit. He didn't wear a ring, and she remembered noticing that and feeling it was enough to decide he couldn't be married, especially with the way he would show up at her job and call her.

She didn't even get a chance to look around much because they ended up in his apartment unexpectedly, meaning it wasn't on the agenda of their date. And now that she thought more about it, she thought that he must have had it on his agenda all along. Joan got up and scanned the room and it seemed like things started to appear that were evidence of a woman having been there. She climbed out of the bed and quickly threw her shirt on and ran to the bathroom that was in the bedroom. She stood there completely amazed, as it was immediately evident that a woman lived in that apartment.

"What the fuck? How could you bring me here!? Are you trying to get me killed?" She was furious, more at herself than anything else. She stomped over to the bed and accidentally kicked over some framed pictures that were stacked under the bed. She leaned down to see what it was that she had kicked over.

"You hid her pictures?"

Joan was flabbergasted that he had gone through that trouble before picking her up. *What kind of man is this?* she wondered.

Charles began mumbling something about putting the pictures under there a while ago because he didn't want to look at them. Joan felt heat rising to the top of her head, and she quickly put her clothes on and asked him to take her home. "And I mean now!" she shouted.

Charles had approached Joan one day as she was working in the neighborhood store and she smiled at him just like she did to almost everyone who came in the store. People were attracted to her naturally anyway, so she didn't think it was odd that this guy came over smilingly to buy some candy. He wasn't the first man who had decided her smile was an invitation. After he bought the candy, he asked her what her name was. She answered, and then quickly and skillfully moved the conversation by asking him if he was registered to vote. She would do things like this to try to let guys know she wasn't flirting, but just being friendly.

But Charles was quite persistent. She did register him to vote, and then he left the store. Five minutes later he came back and asked her if she needed a ride home. She declined his offer because she had a car there. Then he asked for her phone number, which she declined to give him. Then she looked at his hands and saw no wedding band, so she figured he was not married. *Mistake number one,* she thought as they headed out the door to his car.

"But if I had told you I was married when I met you, you wouldn't have talked to me" he said as they got in the car.

She was disgusted and wanted to tell him to shut up, but she let him go on. And he went on to explain stereotypically that he was having problems with his wife, and that they were separated. He claimed that she hadn't moved out yet because she was trying to set something up with her sister, but it began to sound like *whomp whomp whomp* to her as his words droned on, until she finally interrupted to say, "That is no excuse!"

She reflected on how, after more light flirtatious conversation from him and her resistance at the store where they first met, she told him he could call her at the store if he wanted to talk to her. She figured that would put him off, but it didn't. Two days later, he called the store and asked to speak to her. Charles was baffled by the fact that she wouldn't give him her phone number. He said he was calling from his job and wanted to stop by the store to pick her up so they could go for a ride. He said he wanted to get to know her. She made up some excuse and declined. When she left the store, he was sitting in his car in the parking lot.

Now, she couldn't deny that she was flattered by this pursuit. And he was a really good looking guy (which should have been another clue, she decided.) But she convinced him that she had somewhere to go that night and that she could not go for a ride with him. They talked for a little while in the parking lot, and she was beginning to feel her shield weaken because of his smile and attention.

Joan found herself thinking about him more and more, and she even decided that maybe he was alright since he had a job and a car. She was so tired of meeting men who didn't have a driver's license for whatever reason, and she had met many of them. *And he has a job! And he has a nice smile,* she thought to herself as she kept toying with the idea of maybe letting him in.

She really didn't want to let him in because she had just gotten out of a relationship with a man that she grew apart from. He was an older and insecure man who constantly told her that he knew she would leave him for a younger man. Joan never wanted that to be true, especially since that wasn't the reason she grew tired of him. The fact was that she just wasn't satisfied sexually with this man, and she felt very bad about it. She didn't even know how to tell him because he was so good to her in almost every other way. But her frustration and the fact that she wouldn't tell him how tired she was of his 'limp little dick' led her to picking fights with him for other reasons. She kept thinking about trying to suggest using Viagra to this old man, and was shocked that he never thought of it on his own.

She didn't know a man's penis could be so small until she met this old man either. And still, she tried to hang in there with this older man, and did, for a little over three years. He was an expert at oral sex, and she understood why. But that was short-lived compensation, because she craved the feeling of that warm thickness and penetration.

Joan's frustration came to be expressed in other ways, and they began arguing over things that previously seemed trivial. And then he finally started giving her reasons to leave him by hanging out more at the bar with his buddies and getting drunk. She began to see the light at the end of the tunnel with him. Before this, she just could not figure out how to leave him without hurting his feelings. He was

58

an older man, and had repeatedly told her that he suspected she would leave him for a younger man, and he really was wrong about that. She began to think that maybe he kept saying this because he was in denial about the real reason he suspected she would leave him. Either way, she didn't want him to be right about her leaving him for a younger man because it wasn't his age that bothered her. Yet, she didn't have the courage to tell him what was really wrong.

The old man began standing her up— he would go out with his buddies after work and never make it to her apartment. Joan would be furious, and she just added these incidents up to reach the crescendo she was building to. And then finally she told him they had to part ways, and simply ran down the list of reasons. She never said that sex with him was just too frustrating— she couldn't bring herself to tell him even then. He accused her of seeing someone else, and that wasn't true, yet here it was about three weeks after she had that conversation with her old man, and she was already contemplating checking out this guy who was in hot pursuit of her at the store.

Joan justified her clouded judgment to get with Charles by considering the long-term sexual frustration caused by the relationship she had just gotten out of. Charles continued to call and come by the store for another couple of weeks, and they would talk and laugh, and finally she agreed to go out with him. He drove to a park that was in another city and they walked through the park, and she thought that was nice. They talked, and then, under a tree, he pulled her to him and kissed her with the most passionate kiss she had had in a while (and there was the crux of the problem, she figured.) They stared at each other, and she all of a sudden let her guard down and was ready for more. But, she put the brakes on after more embracing, and back to his car they went, and he took her home.

The next night, their juices still flowing from the night before, Charles called her at the store, picked her up, and they went to a nice restaurant for dinner. When they got into his car afterward, he drove off in a direction unfamiliar to her, and as it turned out, they were headed for his apartment. He parked, and before she could even reach for the door handle, he was at her door, opening it. *Gee, a gentleman!* she was thinking as she stepped out of his car. Joan followed him to the door, and he fumbled around with the keys and then finally opened it. Both of them were a little nervous, as this was all happening so fast, yet they both wanted each other really badly by now.

And making love with one another was—unfortunately— even better than either of them thought it would be. It was phenomenal— fantastic!

So her mind boggled as she pondered the statement he had just made, *You know I'm married*, right after the most fantastic orgasm she had ever had.

She turned to look at him as he drove, and he glanced over with a sheepish grin on his face. He began to apologize, but she told him to just shut up. She asked him how he could withhold information like that, and why would he do this to his wife. He went through the stereotypical diatribe again about how he and his wife were having problems and were separating.

The fact was that it wasn't even the first time he had done this to his wife. Yet, he knew his wife would find herself forgiving him, because usually once she allowed him to have sex with her, she would decide that he loved her and wanted her. And then his wife would tear herself down by convincing herself that he must have stepped out because she had done something wrong.

Charles' wife cried to a girlfriend of hers when he moved out one time, and she decided it was because she had gained weight. He came back one night after being gone for about three weeks, driving his girlfriend's car, and his wife allowed him to spend the night. He told her he was considering moving back in with her, and she was so happy that she forgot she was even mad that he was driving the other woman's car. His wife felt wanted again, and felt like she had won him back from that other woman. Never once did she consider that he made this choice because the other woman did not want to take him on full-time with all his baggage. And he did eventually move back in with his wife, and they stayed together for years until she finally mustered up the strength to leave him.

His wife left because she found out that he had never stopped seeing that girlfriend whose car he was driving before he moved back in. She made that discovery after he had been in a car accident and ended up in the hospital. She walked in and saw flowers there with a card where his girlfriend had had the nerve to put her name. Charles lied and told her it was a business associate, but his wife knew better. Charles' wife left him after that, and as soon as he got out of the hospital, the girlfriend left him hanging too. He quickly met another woman and began bringing her to his apartment about a month after his wife moved out. He got so comfortable that he left the new girlfriend there in the bed one morning and went to work. Meanwhile, his wife decided to unexpectedly stop by the apartment to pick up more of her clothes and things she had left behind. She used her key and went right inside. The new girlfriend heard the door open and saw a reflection of Charles' wife in the mirror. She ran to hide in the closet.

Charles' wife went directly to the closet and tried to open the door, but she couldn't get it open. She pulled on it again, and this time she saw a hand attached to the inside doorknob, which startled her. She jumped back in shock and then realized what was going on. She began to scream, "Get out of my closet you whore!" but the woman would not let go of that doorknob. Finally his wife gave up and just left. The woman came out of the closet and grabbed her clothes and ran out the door and she never looked back.

Charles decided that there was no use in revealing these other events to Joan because he felt that his wife was at fault for coming to the house without letting him know. She had left, after all, and had not come back for a month, even though the reason was because she knew he was cheating on her.

So as he continued to drive, he went on with his story, stating that his wife would be moving out soon, and that he'd had a strong attraction to Joan since the first time he saw her working in the store. He then told her he wanted to see her again, and apologized again for bringing her to his apartment without telling her about his soon-to-be ex-wife, as he put it. She was completely mad, and she was even madder because she wanted him. She felt like her head was spinning when he finally pulled up to her apartment. She began to think about it, and decided that this affair would be temporary. She convinced herself that she would not fall in love with him. She turned to him and told him this, and he said Okay and then asked her when he could see her again. She hesitantly said, "Call me." She was feeling very torn and rotten about the whole thing. She hated the idea of being with someone's husband. But he did say they were separating.

Charles called her the next day at the store, and Joan told him to not come there. She was really wrestling with her feelings about this. She had been starving for that tremendous 'sexual healing' feeling she had with Charles, after getting out of the most sexually frustrating relationship she had ever been in with the old man. So now here she was, sweating over a man who had made her see stars in one of the most climactic orgasms she had ever had... *And his ass is married. Damn!*

When she left the store, there he was as usual, sitting there smiling. She melted and walked right over to his car.

"What are you doing here?"

"I had to see you" he said.

She felt all tingly inside, something she hadn't felt in years, just standing there talking to him. *This is a curse,* she thought to herself as she found herself climbing into his car where they eventually embraced and had the best kisses in the world, as he put it. And off to a sleazy, short-stay motel they went. She decided that she could keep her distance better if she didn't let him come to her apartment. But she did finally give him her phone number that night.

And this went on for months, and although she was not proud to be a mistress of this man, she realized after learning more about him that she did not want him to leave his wife because she was afraid that he would want to move in with her. She had no desire to take this man on full-time. The more she found out about him, the more she realized that she could never encourage this man to leave his wife. Charles was his wife's problem, and she was not willing to bring his mountain of issues into her life. He had a mountain of back child support he was paying on, which meant he was usually broke because he didn't make that much money to begin with. The problem was that there was something about him that kept her drawn to him, especially in the safety of her buffer zone, the buffer zone being her refusal to give him a key to her place or to allow him to come there much. Charles asked her for a key once, but she told him no, and said that he could not have a key as long as he was married.

Charles' wife did not particularly love him in a way that made her want to just run up and kiss him when they were together, but whenever he did decide to have sex with her, she decided that he still loved her. Sex between them had really degraded to a duty she provided as his wife on the occasions when he desired it. Most of the time, he didn't even sleep in the same room with her, and he told her it was because she snored. His wife became so insecure that she could not imagine her life without him in it, even if only to be able to appear married to her family and friends. They were young when they got married, and she felt very proud to have him with her because he was so light-skinned and tall. He already had two children before she married him, and then after repeated cheating incidents over the years, their relationship had suffered, and she held an angry grudge that allowed her to use guilt as a weapon against him. They both made excuses to themselves as to why they stayed together, including the fact that they were just used to each other and that they had three children together. Their youngest daughter had a half-brother that was the same age as her because he had gotten another woman pregnant around the same time his wife got pregnant the last time.

The outrage his wife felt once she learned about the other child sent her into a raging storm. Their new baby was only one month old when this particular girlfriend had hers. He ended up telling his wife because he wanted to see his new son. She screamed for him to leave, but he wouldn't leave, and she knew he wouldn't. She hated the fact that she loved him, and she hated the fact that she loved having a husband that looked like him. She hated the fact that she did not want to let him go and end up like so many women she knew who had no man.

But how much of this could she take? His wife would wonder many times on that. She knew Charles was not faithful and that he never had been, even before they got married. He promised her convincingly that he would never cheat on her again when she agreed to marry him. At that time he was unemployed, and they were already living together and had had a son two years before that, anyway. He had soon found a job though, and then they went to the Justice of the Peace and got married. This made his wife feel that he had finally changed, and she was very hopeful about their family.

And that was why his wife was so outraged when he revealed to her that he had another child who was born one month after his wife had their baby daughter. His wife was so hurt at learning about the other child that she packed some things and moved in with her mother for a short while. And it was only a short while because she began to miss him, and he knew how to pour on the charm. Charles was confident that he could get her to come back, and knew he only needed to give her a little time to cool off. But his wife came back a bit more ferocious after learning about the other child. She had a fury inside that was evident in her aura. Forgiveness was not complete this time, but it was overridden by her desire to have him in her life. She demanded that he have nothing whatsoever to do with the other child, and he agreed, but by this time he had seen his other child while his wife was with her mother. He needed his wife to move back in so she could help with the bills and rent, so he was prepared to agree to just about anything. She knew his need, and she decided to feel sorry for him, which was ludicrous, but it became part of her justification for getting back together with him.

The woman who had his son, discovered after they started seeing each other, that he was married, and she decided to keep up the affair for a while. When she got pregnant, she had already decided that she would keep the child. She did not want Charles to leave his wife either, and when she told him she was pregnant, he almost seemed happy. He stood there and said, "I knew it!" and then asked her what she planned to do about it. She told him that she planned to keep the baby, but that she did not plan to pursue anything from him. She told him to go on and be with his wife, as if she had him pegged to be her sperm donor. He was shocked and almost insulted at the way she dismissed him. She knew that his wife had just had their baby. What Charles didn't know was that she was making plans to move out of the state. And she let him know the day she was leaving with his son, and he put up a minor argument about not being able to see his child if she moved away. But it all kind of fell in place once his wife got back since she demanded that he not have anything to do with the other child.

So here it was, years later, and he had stepped out again, in his familiar charade. Charles had never worn his wedding band, and his wife never put up too much fuss about that. *His wife should have forced him to wear his ring*, Joan thought as she opened her door to let him in one day when he came by after work. By now, they were through playing games such as him meeting her at the store she worked at, and she went ahead and gave him her address. He immediately began to come to her apartment—a lot—whenever he got the chance. He had told his wife he was going to see one of his buddies who covered for him all the time when he decided to see her.

Joan began to feel a little uncomfortable as he became more comfortable. He began demanding that she call him on his cell phone or at his house when he told her his wife wouldn't be home. Joan couldn't understand his demanding that she call him at home, because his wife was back in the apartment full-time again. This was an argument they would have periodically because she kept telling him that it made no sense to take chances like that. In reality, she just didn't want to increase her violation that way. She felt it was bad enough that she was in a relationship with this woman's husband. Joan just wanted to draw a line somewhere. So the day that he had finally convinced her to call him one afternoon when he stayed home from work, he learned why it was a bad idea.

He knew she would be getting her nails done that afternoon because she was off that day from work, and he decided to take the day off for another reason, which included getting a chance to see Joan. Charles insisted that she call him as soon as she was done at the nail salon, which she did, reluctantly. He met her in an inconspicuous place, parked his car and got in hers, and off they went to a sleazy short-stay motel, just for the thrill of it. After phenomenal, mind blowing, orgasmic sex that brought them both to the point of gazing into each other's eyes and knowing they were terribly hooked on each other, they finally got up and got out of there. And she was feeling all giddy like she was walking on air as both of them went their separate ways. And then she realized there were messages on her cell phone. She hadn't even heard it ring. When she listened, she was outraged to find out it was his wife. He had forgotten to clear the caller ID before he left. This beautiful afternoon that had left her in such a good mood ended up being abruptly ruined in a traumatic way. She was shaken by the torrent of names she was called as his wife cursed her out without even taking a breath, ending with "Stay your fuckin' ass away from my husband!" Somehow, Charles was able to calm his wife down about this once again with another obvious lie.

After getting past that bump in the road, Joan enjoyed having him around on her terms. She did not want him in her life full-time because he was a controlling and, in some ways, immature man. Beyond making passionate love the way they had been for months, she did find that she wanted more out of their relationship, but not enough to push him to leave his wife and bring him into her life with all of his baby mama drama and financial baggage. There were times that she wanted to take him along on some vacations with her, but he was always afraid, and also he could not afford it. Even when she told him she could cover the expenses, he wasn't comfortable doing that.

On rare occasions Charles managed to spend some time with her on various holidays, but she seemed to always feel that he had to leave too soon. He began to leave his cell phone in his car because his wife would start calling soon after he got there as if she had some kind of intuition regarding his whereabouts. Joan became conscious that she had to remind herself that she was very successful and owned her home and that she just did not need him moving in with his drama and baggage, and she realized her freedom in that regard, which made her feel a little better. She also felt that she'd feel a lot better had she never started this relationship with Charles. She was glad that she never gave him a key to her apartment.

It was weird how she and the wife kept this going for years, staying way out of each other's ways. And as it seemed, everyone was getting what they wanted out of the deal—somewhat.

Just An Illusion

6

"I'm letting her live in my apartment because she ain't got nowhere else to go," Jamal said after finally convincing his latest prey to let him move into her place.

Like a woman in a perpetual functional coma, Jackie heard him, and yet didn't hear him. She accepted his excuse and only thought about her fantasy— that he wanted her. At fifty-two years old, this thirty-eight year old man wanted her. Jackie heard Jamal, but she heard that he wanted to move into her place. That meant to her that he would be with her. It meant that he wanted to be with her, and that made her feel complete. She knew he had some baby mama drama going on, but he explained it as a situation where the baby's mama had nowhere to go, so they were just living as roommates.

Jackie felt good about this man wanting her. She was proud to show Jamal off around her friends because he actually knew how to act in public. He was young and good looking and she could bring him to banquets and everything! So she didn't mind that he was usually broke and that she had to pay for those kinds of outings. Jamal knew how to play the role, and he did it well to secure his position in Jackie's life. He even went to her family reunion picnic with her, and when her cousin gave a toast, he asked all the men who had told their woman they loved her that day to stand. Jamal stood up immediately. Jackie couldn't remember him saying it, but she was just thrilled that he stood up for everyone to see.

So now she was finally getting him into her apartment so they could truly live in a committed relationship. Jamal dragged his huge, dark green Hefty trash bag full of clothes up the stairs, into the apartment Jackie was renting, and into the bedroom that he had already spent numerous nights in. Jackie was very happy to have her man moving in. She had prepared dinner and had decided that they were going to live like a real family. She had already become proficient in ignoring the baby mama drama he had left behind in "his" apartment.

She had already been driving Jamal to work in the morning whenever he spent the night. Now that Jamal had moved in, it had become part of her morning routine. Jackie hadn't thought about that on the day he told her he was moving in. But after a month into this situation, she was growing a little tired of getting up extra early to take him to work in her hoopty piece of car. *He ain't even fixin' his mouth to suggest that he plans on getting his own ride*, she lamented.

"You know, you should think about buying a car so you can take yourself to work in the morning. It's really getting to be a bit much for me. Or, you should think about taking the bus in like you take home."

"What? Oh! Now you tired of taking me to work? Damn! I knew you was gonna front on me like this."

Jackie was pissed off that he reacted like that. He just wasn't trying to make anything easier for her. She thought that by moving in, he would help her by paying some of the rent and bills, but so far—nothing. Jamal had not offered up one dime. He had brought food home a couple of times for her to cook though, and she was always flattered and appreciative, as though it was special.

Jackie had no idea that Jamal's license had been suspended for years now because of tickets that he had not paid. He rarely asked to drive her car anyway, but when he did, sometimes she let him. She just didn't think he would be asking for her car if he had no license. He didn't push it, though, on the occasions that she refused to let him drive her car. She wasn't really into allowing him to drive her car because she needed it to get to work, and because, in the back of her mind, she knew he was the irresponsible type.

So Jackie continued to drive him to work every morning, and finally, she asked him for gas money one morning.

"I ain't got no extra money. You know I need money to take the bus home. Damn!"

Jamal noticed Jackie's anger, but wasn't really too concerned. He just decided she wanted him to sex her up at night, and so far, it had been all to his benefit since he had nowhere else to live. The idea that she might put him out hadn't even crossed his mind. He figured his lie about allowing his baby's mama to stay in

68

"his" apartment would work in his favor, giving the appearance that he had a place to go if he chose to.

Kicking him out hadn't crossed Jackie's mind either. She dropped him off and thought about approaching him regarding what he does with his money when he came in after work that night. She was thinking that she never made anything clear with him before he moved in as to how she expected him to participate financially. The idea that she was working two jobs and he was contributing nothing was getting on her nerves. But the sex was good, and she loved having him in her bed at night. At least she was not like so many of her girlfriends who didn't have a man. *What to do… what to do…*

Jackie met Jamal in the bar she worked at on the weekends. So she figured that he spent a lot of his money on drinking with friends and the weed he smoked on occasion. But she decided that she must ask him, because now they were months into this living arrangement, and she was realizing the burden of "keeping" him more and more.

The night that she decided to confront him, he actually came home right after work at around 7:00 p.m. She fixed him something to eat because she had not yet put what she cooked away; this was her usual routine, since she never knew what time he might come in. She normally fixed him a plate and wrapped it and sat it on the stove so that if he came in after she was in bed, he only had to toss it into the microwave. Jamal ate and then grabbed a beer and plopped down onto the couch in their living room in front of the TV. Jackie sat down next to him on the couch and kissed him on the cheek. He slid down so that he could lean his head back, and moved into a more relaxed position by putting his feet up on the coffee table. She leaned down and rested her head on his shoulder and managed to get comfortable on him. She then mustered up the courage to tell him that she needed help with the bills and that since he was living there, she wanted him to contribute. She told him that they could open a bank account just for bills in both of their names.

He sat up so abruptly that her head fell down behind his back on the couch. He just looked at her for a few seconds without saying anything. In his mind, this arrangement of being with this older woman meant she was going to take care of him. And anyway, this was how he had been living since he left his mama's house. He had never had to be responsible and never had to learn to be accountable.

69

He thought about trying to go back to his baby's mama, but he knew she had had her fill of him and there was no going back there. He thought about how he had lied about it, saying that it was his apartment and that he was allowing his baby's mama to live there.

"Well what you want from me? I only bring home three hundred dollars a week, and you know I'm paying child support."

He was lying about that too. He was really bringing home four hundred dollars per week and he wasn't paying any child support. The baby's mama hadn't even bothered to file for it. Jamal always claimed to his friends and anyone who asked or was in earshot when the subject came up that he was paying child support as if it were some kind of badge of honor or obligation deserving of praise.

"Three hundred dollars? But what are you doing with it? You don't have a car... are you saving some money?"

"Yeah," he said, lying. He claimed he brought it to his mother to put in the bank for him. In reality, he had never had a bank account. He was always buying clothes, liquor, and weed, and sometimes gambled on the pool table at the bar he hangs out at. He never had any money left over from his pay.

"Well you're going to have to stop bringing money to your mother and take care of some things here where you're living at! It's only fair."

Jackie thought about telling him to go back and live in his own apartment with his baby's mama, and it seemed like he read that thought on her face. He immediately realized that his lie could catch up to him about that, and in desperation said that he would give her some money at the end of the week when he got paid. So Jamal agreed that he would give her $75 per week, reluctantly. Jackie felt triumphant and was really happy about the agreement.

Two weeks later, Jackie's car broke down. By this time, he had given her one $75 contribution, because on the first Friday, he had made an excuse as to why he couldn't pay.

"We need another car," she told him after getting home from riding with a coworker. She had to leave her car in the parking lot of her job, which was where it had broken down. She was lucky to even get there, and once she pulled into the parking lot something blew, and she managed to roll into a parking spot.

70

Now this was getting to be too much, he thought. But then he thought about how comfortable he was there in her place too. There wasn't too much responsibility, and he got all he needed for $75 per week. But now he had to take the bus to work in the morning. That meant he had to get up extra early, and it was going to cost him more money. He was very mad about this inconvenience. He didn't mind taking the bus home much, because many times he stopped off to go to the club where his buddies hung out at before going home. Jackie never complained that he came in late, and he never understood why, either. His younger girlfriend, the baby's mama, was always mad about that. He still considered his baby's mama to be his girlfriend since he still stopped by there to jump off into a sex romp with her every once in a while. She usually let him, too, because in her mind it was a booty call, and he was her baby's father, after all. She never let him stay overnight anymore though, because she didn't want to feel like she was actually with him. The baby's mama had finally had it with him after he stole her car while she was asleep and then got into an accident. She had to end up getting him out of jail, paying the fines and towing charge as well as a surcharge on her insurance that included a huge premium increase. That was her last straw.

Meanwhile, Jamal had no clue that this fifty-two-year-old woman enjoyed her quiet time after work. And the fact that he came home in time for her to feel him in her bed at night was the fix she felt she required. Jackie was annoyed with her situation though, because in the back of her mind, she felt pathetic.

Somehow she managed to get an old, beat-up car from a friend on a five hundred dollar IOU. She was shocked that Jamal gave her one hundred dollars toward the car, which cost six hundred dollars. What she didn't realize was that he would feel ownership of the car based on that, and that he would begin asking to drive it. Jackie considered it a mild inconvenience since he didn't ask to use it on the weekdays. She would get up as usual and take him to work, and he would take the bus home. But he had asked to use it on the weekend a couple of times, saying that he wanted to go to the store, and had then stayed out for hours.

Then one night, she got a call from the police station. He had been in an accident with the car. The car was registered in her name, and the insurance was in her name. She got to the police station and found out that he had no driver's license. She was furious. The

71

accident was a fender bender, but the car was impounded, and she had to borrow money from her daughter to get it out. Meanwhile, he was released on his own recognizance when she got there, and it was déjà vu for him, so he said nothing as they went to pick the car up.

They climbed into her daughter's car and she was embarrassed and pissed off that her daughter was there to bear witness to the fact that her mother had picked up another loser. Still, he said nothing. Jackie's daughter dropped them off at the tow lot and left. Once Jackie and Jamal got home, she asked him why he would do such a thing.

"Why would you take chances with my car?"

He had the nerve to say, "It's our car! I paid for it too."

She was done. She went into the bedroom and just fell backward onto the bed. He sat out in the living room and then got nervous because he thought she might be contemplating forcing him out of the apartment. So he got up and went into the bedroom and lay down next to her and begged her forgiveness while kissing her, and she melted because she felt that he loved her. Back to fantasyland she went as she rolled over in his embrace and she asked him to not drive their car anymore. He agreed at that moment, and she believed him.

TKO

7

"Bitch! I'll kill you!" he yelled after he punched her in the face right in front of everybody at the bar.

Tricia had been sitting there for about an hour, having drinks and laughing with friends she hadn't seen in a long while. She was very surprised to see a girlfriend she had gone to high school with there, and that compelled her to have a seat and a drink, since her friend from back when bought it for her. And then others at the bar bought rounds and she ended up staying longer than she had intended. Her boyfriend, Ronald, was enraged beyond control when he found her sitting there laughing and talking as if she hadn't just taken his last $20 out of his wallet and found and smoked his last rock of crack, which he thought he had hidden from her.

Tricia held her hand over her eye, which was swelling up fast as her girlfriend dragged her away from the bar and toward the door. Others had wrestled Ronald down to the floor while the bartender called the police. Her high school girlfriend was outraged, and she asked Tricia what the hell was wrong with that man. Tricia knew that her girlfriend would never understand how she could stay with Ronald, who kicked her ass regularly—so regularly that when she arrived at her girlfriend's apartment, all she could say was, "I gotta get him out," meaning that she was worried about him sitting in jail overnight and not about her swollen black eye.

Her girlfriend found an ice pack buried in her freezer which was really supposed to be used in a cooler, wrapped it in a towel, and gave it to her. Tricia placed it on her eye and had an annoyed look on her face because of the whole thing. Her face had an expression of contemplation instead of pain and distress. It was all about getting Ronald out of jail.

It was amazing that the two of them managed to stay together all these years to begin with. Tricia appeared to be cheating on

73

Ronald all the time, but the real situation was that he had become her personal pimp by allowing her to be with other men as long as she gained something from it. And then he pretended like he believed there was no sex involved in these transactions. It was hard for Tricia's high school girlfriend whom she had grown up with to imagine what she had turned into. Her girlfriend also knew that since Tricia's lifestyle was so unsavory, there was no way she could allow her to stay longer than overnight. So she asked Tricia, before even pulling out her futon, where she would go in the morning, because she just did not want to believe she'd be going back to her man's apartment. But that was exactly where Tricia was planning to go once she figured out how to get him out of jail.

"I deserved it. I took something from him— I knew he'd be mad— I lost track of time" Tricia lamented.

"Are you kidding me? No one deserves that kind of violence! What has happened to you?"

Tricia sat down and continued talking as if her friend wasn't even there.

"I have to get Ronald out in the morning because he has to go to work."

Her girlfriend could not understand the mentality that was necessary for Tricia to believe she deserved to be punched in the eye. But that's what she believed. What Tricia's girlfriend didn't realize was that Tricia had grown to expect his reaction when she did certain things, like take money out of his wallet or do his drugs after she ran out of her own. His violence was getting worse, though, and more frequent. She believed he would kill her one day, and that was something that she actually accepted.

He had almost killed her once after he had lost his job. Ronald had begun stealing equipment from the facility he worked at to sell it on the street. He had sunk down into Tricia's world and had become heinous and evil about it too. It was deep-rooted anger, borne from the notion he had about where he was headed, and he subconsciously knew it wasn't good. However, he chose not to stop the downward spiral, and instead was more enthralled with keeping her, no matter what. So when he finally got home after selling the TV he stole from the basement of one of the buildings he worked in and found that she had not only spent the money he had put aside for their rent, but also hadn't saved him a hit of the crack she had obviously been smoking, he went berserk. He threw her around the room and then into the empty bathtub after tearing her clothes off. He picked up a pair of scissors and tried to ram them into her vagina, but she was screaming and holding his arms with all of her might. He then threw the scissors down and she lay in the bathtub, out of breath from the struggle. He turned the water on and the tub began to fill as she lay there panting and gasping for air through her sobs until there was enough to cover her head. Tricia thought he was done so she didn't move while the water was flowing into the tub. She started forward as he pushed her head down when she realized he was going to drown her in the bathtub. She struggled and scratched his arms so deeply that his blood colored the water as it dispersed in the turbulence as he continued to push her head down into it. Somehow she flipped around, and he banged her head on the side of the old porcelain bathtub, which caused her to slither down into the water in a state of unconsciousness.

Ronald watched her lifeless body slide down into the bloody water that was becoming more deeply red with the blood that was running from her split lip. But then he suddenly realized that he may have killed her. He snatched her up out of the water, splashing it all over the floor and toilet, and pulled her out of the bathtub. He noticed that her nose was also bleeding, so he laid her on the floor and ran to get some ice to wrap in a towel. When he got back to the bathroom, she had regained consciousness. He wiped her bleeding face and held the ice that he had wrapped in a towel on her face and began to cry. She began to cry too as she hoisted herself up using the toilet as an anchor. She held onto the sink and looked into the mirror and immediately knew that her nose was broken. It wasn't the first time.

Ronald had been working in the dietary department of the nursing home for over twenty years. But when he met up with Tricia, she was already living a life of total dysfunction through the use of drugs—specifically heroin, which she liked to sniff, but crack would do, as well as anything else she could get her hands on if her drug of choice wasn't available. When he ran into her, he was thrilled, because they had known each other years ago and had even gone out on a few dates back then. So he was really happy to bump into her again as she was visiting someone at the nursing home.

Tricia always attracted a lot of men because she was tall, slim, very light skinned, and had long wavy hair, but somehow she was never smart enough to use these attributes to her advantage past a level of survival. Ronald had no clue what he was in for when he ran into her that day. Instead, he was swept up by the fact that she accepted his date offer. He didn't even bother to ask her what she had been doing with herself during all the years that had passed since he had last seen her.

They went out to eat the night she ran into him at the nursing home, and then she asked him to bring her to one of her regular nightclub stops. The place was a total dive, yet she had no problem asking him to go there because she also wanted to see where his head was at. He obliged, and after they got there she introduced him to some people she knew in there, and finally got around to telling him she wanted a "toot" and was going to pick up some coke. She played it off as if she bought it occasionally just to sniff sometimes while she was out having a drink. He told her that he didn't mind having a toot every now and then as it turned out, so he was okay with it, and they sat there for the rest of the night taking turns going to the restrooms for their toot. Actually, Ronald hadn't had any cocaine in over ten years, but he figured there was no harm in a recreational toot every once in a while.

They began seeing each other regularly after that night, and Ronald eventually started finding out more negative things about Tricia. But instead of breaking off the relationship when the red flags were waving and slapping him in the face, he decided he could fix her. He was so thrilled to have someone who looked like her that he didn't want to let her go.

It wasn't long after they met at the nursing home that Tricia left the friend's house she was living at, where she slept on the couch, to quickly move into Ronald's apartment. And it wasn't long after that that he lost his job and they ended up moving into his mother's house. Ronald's mother was the cushion he usually fell on over the years and she was always there to pick up his slack. He knew it would not be a problem to move in. He didn't feel that he overly took advantage of his mother, but he knew that he could if he wanted to because he knew his mother had some guilt about the fact that she never allowed him to know his father—at least he blamed her for his not knowing him, anyway. He'd only throw that in her face during desperate times, but there was no need this time. His mother seemed resigned to just letting him come in and stay in the bedroom he had slept in as a child. Bringing his girlfriend in was just something incidental in her mind, and she just had no energy to protest his request, which involved bringing his girlfriend along.

The problem was that he didn't just lose his job—his employer decided to prosecute him for theft since they had him on tape carrying items out of the place. He ended up going to prison for a year, and while he was there, Tricia visited him regularly, but she also kept her lifestyle going like the street expert she was. She managed to hook up with another man who had completely lost his mind over her. He had the physical characteristics of a frog, and although in the back of his mind he knew he had to have money to have a woman who looked like her with him, he always deluded himself into believing otherwise. And even when it became plainly evident that she was with him because of what he could do for her, he didn't care. He just wanted Tricia to be with him, and he didn't care that she was using him. She stayed with him at his house sometimes, but there were many times that she never made it to his place because she was stuck in the crack house she went to where someone usually came by ready to get high. Occasionally, she'd go back to Ronald's mother's house.

The crack house was so hot one summer day when Tricia was there that the couple who lived there managed to run an extension cord from someone's apartment in the building next door so that the cord went out of their window, across the alley, and into their neighbor's window in order to plug in their refrigerator and a fan. The woman's husband had concocted some sort of Flintstone-style air conditioner by hanging a bag of ice in front of the fan, and it actually blew cool air! Tricia was shocked at the ingenuity of a drug addict. The place was overrun with roaches and mice. She would have considered that she was high when she saw a mouse climbing up the curtain, except she had just gotten there that day and hadn't even had a blast yet. She stayed in this calamity of an apartment for a few hours and finally decided she had had enough because she kept finding roaches in her clothes. She had not ever forgiven them for the time she found roaches in her hair when she passed out and they left her lying on the floor next to the couch as they continued to smoke up her rocks.

Tricia went back to The Frog's house, and he was mad when she got there. He was always annoyed that she went missing for hours and sometimes days at a time, but he would quickly get over it and be glad she was there. When she arrived from the crack house, she went to the bathroom and took a shower and realized that her ear was swollen and hurting. She tried to stick her fingernail into it, but the canal was almost closed. She figured she had sweated so much in that furnace of a crack house with the ice bag air conditioner, that she had developed an ear infection. She mashed on the side of her ear and it felt puffy and it hurt. The next morning, she saw some pus on her pillow, so she got up and went into the bathroom to get a paper towel, which she twisted so that she could try and stick it in there, but she had no luck. The Frog got up and saw her leaning on the bathroom sink while peering into the mirror as she tried to push the paper towel into her ear. He saw how swollen her ear was and asked her if she needed to go to the hospital, but she declined. When he got home from work, she tearfully told him that she had pushed her finger into her ear and her fake nail had popped off inside and she couldn't get it out. So The Frog took Tricia to the hospital emergency center where they managed to get her fingernail out along with the embedded roaches that had hatched in her ear and caused the infection that was eating a hole through her eardrum. The drainage was so foul that it even made the doctor gasp. The Frog was outraged and horrified at the same time. He forbade her from ever going wherever she had been again. He had already been complaining about her bringing roaches to his house.

Meanwhile, The Frog knew about Tricia's man in jail, and he knew it was getting close to the time that her man was going to get out. He was reminded by the fact that she began spending more time at Ronald's mother's house. She had told Ronald about The Frog, but explained him as another man she did house cleaning for. She had already been claiming to be a housekeeper for another man who lived about sixty miles away and was an owner of a hardware store before she and Ronald had gotten together. She met him in a bar one night and she pushed up on him enough after he bought her numerous drinks that he ended up bringing her to his home. She had been in this housekeeping/sexual relationship for years. After a while, the relationship became more about her housekeeping duties, and she began going there to wash his clothes, change linen on his bed, clean bathrooms, etc., while he was at work.

Once Ronald finally got out of jail, they lived at his mother's house as if he had never left. The Frog was particularly put out over this and was begging her regularly whenever he could get to her. Since Ronald had nothing, she easily convinced him to allow her to see The Frog and the other guy so that she could clean their apartments for money. Ronald knew in the back of his mind what was probably occurring between her and these men, but he decided to go along with the housekeeping story and considered it necessary until he got a job.

Tricia managed to convince The Frog to let her borrow his car on a few occasions. Sometimes she wouldn't return his car to him for days, and he would be furious because he would end up taking the bus to work. But once she finally returned his car and he saw her, he would put on a front like he was mad, but she would easily calm him down when she unbuckled his belt—an act which brought on his trance. She began taking The Frog's car to pick up Ronald and take him with her to the hardware store owner's house. They would have luxurious sex in that man's bed while he was at work, drink his wine, and have a grand old time. This went on for a while, a couple of times per month, until one day The Frog's car broke down on the highway. Tricia managed to call someone to pick her and Ronald up, and she left The Frog's car on the side of the highway. She didn't even bother to call him to tell him what happened to his car. The Frog did find out by way of a summons in the mail about abandoning his car on the highway, and he was so outraged that he wanted to kill Tricia. He waited and waited for her to contact him as she usually did, but it didn't happen. She left The Frog completely after his car broke down and never contacted him again.

After a while, Ronald found a job, and they managed to get an attic apartment in a run-down neighborhood that was equipped with local and convenient street-peddling drug dealers and other usual riffraff. Ronald was clean when he got out of prison, but by now Tricia had managed to convince him to try a blast and a sniff, and in an instant, it was back to the same madness he had left. And the spiral downward to his paranoid and insane jealousy became even more ferocious, as she would go missing some nights. If she came home with a bag or a rock for him it sometimes smoothed things out. But their nights usually ended with it being all gone, and him calling her all kinds of names— stupid, whore, and low-down bitch that needs her neck broken.

"Look at those bags under your eyes. You look like shit" he would tell her regularly, and then after making sure her feelings were hurt, he would tell her he could say those things because he loved her. He told her she was stupid all the time, and she began saying she knew it out loud.

Ronald had no idea that while he was at work during the day, she was a few blocks away, sucking off strangers when the opportunity presented itself so she could have the drugs she needed and some left for him when he got home, if she made it there at all.

One day after they both barricaded themselves in their attic apartment with the windows nailed shut, the shades down, and towels wedged under the bottom of the door to the hallway outside, they emerged out of the small closet they had been in for about twelve hours while smoking crack. The crack had been gone for about an hour before they managed to come out. She had torn pockets off of clothes that hung behind her thinking that every speck of lint inside might be a rock. He had literally scraped wood from the floorboards with his bare fingernails, digging in crevices with the sharp, broken edge of the burnt up glass stem he had been smoking with.

They crawled out of that closet on their hands and knees, their fingers and hands all black from the soot and ashes that filled the ashtray they had been using and fishing through for rocks. They both seemed to stop at the same time. They looked at each other and then began to cry. It seemed like they both had the same thought at the same time—that they had had enough for the thousandth time. But this time, they decided to find a meeting to help them along.

They made it to a Narcotics Anonymous meeting that night and continued to go for a while. It wasn't until Tricia ran into a friend who was not a true friend but a drug friend who owed her money, that she was lured into the bar one night for what she told herself would be a soda. But then someone she knew sent her a drink and she didn't turn it down. And then she was invited to the restroom. She hesitated, but found herself sliding off the barstool, and like a robot programmed for disaster, she marched right to that restroom, and then the package came out, and then her nose found its way onto the straw that pulled that powder right up into her sinuses, and the familiar bitter drain down her throat landed her back at the crack house that night like she had never left. She found the courage to go home the next day when she thought Ronald would be at work, and she found a note from him telling her to pack her shit and get the hell out. She didn't pack, but sat down on the bed and cried. Once Ronald got home from work, he ranted and stomped and screamed at her, and the minute she opened her mouth to say something, he found his fist in it, without even realizing he had swung at her.

After cleaning up the blood and putting some ice on her face, he apologized and told her he loved her, but added that he could not continue with her if she was going to keep using drugs—that is, until her purse fell to the floor from the snack tray that was next to the bed and he saw her stem roll out, full of residue from smoking crack the night before. He picked it up, sat down on the bed and looked at it. And then he picked up an ink pen and pushed the screen that was filled with the residue of what she had been smoking and saw that it was stuck. So he picked up a cigarette lighter and swirled the flame around the screen and saw the residue begin to melt. He pushed the screen and it slid ever so slowly to the top, collecting a thick pile of crack residue as it approached the edge. He put the stem to his lips and flashed the flame back and forth across the tip of the stem, each time relishing the sizzle and crackle as he pulled thick, white smoke through the glass.

"As the world turns..."

Tricia spent the entire night that her girlfriend brought her home from the bar with a black eye and swollen face trying to figure out how to get Ronald out of jail for hitting her. The next morning, she got up and her girlfriend fixed breakfast and they both sat down and ate without saying much. Tricia felt slightly ashamed that her girlfriend knew she was going right back into the situation of madness with her boyfriend, but that was a fleeting thought that quickly turned to the arrogance of *I don't give a damn what she thinks* floating through her head. With that expression showing on her face and emanating from her being, her girlfriend didn't say much else, and Tricia thanked her girlfriend and left, walking up the street.

81

Mine Eyes

8

"Hey! Send her a drink" Black shouted to the bartender as he continued his loud banter at the other end of the bar.

As Candy sat there at the bar with her usual drink, sitting in her usual seat, she had somehow caught the attention of that loudmouthed man she'd seen there many, many times before. She was very flattered that he bought her that drink, because this was a man who usually ignored her. It didn't even bother her that he normally came in right after work, all dusty and dirty with paint splatters all over his arms. His boots were so beat up and worn that the outward corners of the heels were elevated and didn't even touch the ground anymore when he was standing still. His modus operandi was to burst through the door of the bar, shouting as he came in at his friends, who were usually already there and who were also loud, cussin', rowdy guys. The overall decibel level in the bar was raised once these guys got together.

Candy's reputation preceded her there, and she was considered a mainstay from the neighborhood. This was a neighborhood bar with regulars who took their same barstool positions whenever they were there, which they were on regular, designated nights every week. It seemed baffling to her for a moment that Black had all of a sudden decided to buy her a drink, but she almost immediately put that puzzlement aside and relished in the idea that this man wanted her.

He finally sauntered down to where she was sitting and plopped down onto the barstool next to her. He didn't have much conversation for her other than—

"What you doin' later?" and "Do you want another drink?"

He knew she had nothing to do because he knew she usually sat there at the bar, and that she was usually still there when he left. Sometimes he'd come back later in the same night, and she'd still be there until around 11:00 p.m., at which time she would leave and slither her drunk ass home. She lived just around the block and usually walked to the bar since she lived so close.

After a few drinks, Black had convinced Candy to let him take her home, which really didn't take much convincing. They left the bar that night and he brought her home in his beat up pickup truck, which was the only vehicle she ever saw him drive. He parked his truck right in front of the house she lived in, and leaned over to kiss her. Candy was just bursting inside at the idea of finally having a boyfriend again. She surmised that this man was now her boyfriend, and she was swept up in the moment as he got out of the car, raced around to her side and opened her door, and then followed her to the door of the enclosed front porch. She turned to kiss him goodnight after telling him that she lived there with her mother and grandmother, so he could not come in. After hearing that, he opened the door to the front porch and they both stepped in. He somehow managed to push her down to the floor on the porch while kissing her, and then he pushed himself up inside of her, her right there on the front porch floor. It was late and she didn't even consider that either her mother or grandmother might get up and catch them but it turned out okay, because the whole act didn't last long. It seemed like it hadn't even been five minutes before she snapped back into consciousness at hearing the zipper on his pants going up. She was just climbing up off the floor and Black was already out the door of the front porch as he quietly yelled back without turning his head,

"I'll see ya later," and he barreled on down the stairs, jumped in his truck, and sped off. What registered in her head was that her boyfriend had said he would see her later.

The next day, Candy sat at the bar on her regular barstool and she was all charged up and just waiting for someone to ask her what had happened with Black, because she knew people there had seen them leave together the night before. But no one said anything—not to her, anyway. Just before she got there, the bartender was guffawing with a few others in there about Candy and Black. They could not believe he had left with her, because they all knew how needy and overbearing she was. They were still laughing when she walked through the door, but her ego never allowed her to think they were laughing about her. She sat down and had a proud look on her face, which made them laugh even more.

And not long after she got there, Black came through the door and walked over to the bar and sat next to her, which was something he had never done prior to the night before. He bought Candy a drink and then went on down to the other end of the bar where his loud talking friends lived on their respective barstools. They were cussin' and going on as they usually did about anything and everything. Black didn't say anything else to her until he was ready to leave. He paid his bar tab and hers, and she was thrilled. She figured that she would ask him about his wife when they left. *He must be leaving his wife,* she decided.

Everyone at the bar knew Black was married, including Candy. But the regular men at the bar that had wives kept quiet about each other's infidelities as though it were some kind of "bar code." They embarked on these sex escapades and never told on each other. Nor did they ever try to stop each other or consider these infidelities as really damaging to their home lives. Every now and then a couple of them, in their drunken philosophies, would bring up the fact that their wives never bothered to come to the bar to see what they were doing. But they would stop short of admitting that their wives were probably happy that their husbands were out instead of getting on their nerves at home. These men were not the most dapper of guys to begin with. Some were crusty, dusty, and unkempt. One could only wonder how they managed to find women to marry them in the first place. Their wives' usual complaint was the amount of money they spent at the bar, not the fact that they didn't come home right after work.

Now, the guys at the end of the bar did wonder what had gotten into their friend, who had decided after all these years to all of a sudden indulge in Candy, who sat at the other end of the bar, because they knew what a delusional, ridiculous woman she had always been. But then they all settled on the realization that it was sex, so it made sense because of that.

Black and Candy's next rendezvous was a trip to a nearby forest and into one of the picnic area parking lots. It was pitch black there, and his headlights made all kinds of moths, gnats, mosquitoes, and other bugs visible. There were so many that Candy thought it would be impossible not to breathe them in with every breath. Black parked and turned the lights out and told her that they should take a walk. It didn't even occur to her how familiar this move was to him as she followed along. At a certain clearing not far from a gazebo that was near some trees and an anchored barbecue grill, he grabbed her and kissed her, pushed her down to the ground, and they had sex right there. It was the same move he used on her front porch. This time, since she knew the move, she went down a little easier to the ground.

Once he was done, he jumped up the same way he had the night before and zipped up his pants. She gathered herself, brushing grass and twigs off her clothes and her back, and took some tissues out of her purse to wipe off the messiness he left between her legs. There was so much slime that she decided to leave the wad of tissue in her panties as she pulled them up. She didn't notice him wipe anything. He just pulled his pants up and made his way to the truck and told her to get up and said, "Let's go," because he was getting bitten by mosquitoes.

As they were driving back to her house, she asked him if he wanted her phone number and if he would call her, and then she asked him if he was leaving his wife.

"Hell No! I ain't leavin' my wife! What da hell gave you that idea?"

Candy was shocked at first by the way he answered her. That her boyfriend could talk to her that way was incredulous in her mind. Then she became furious because of the way he answered her. She was thinking that he had to be in love with her because he had bought her drinks and he wanted to make love to her. All the while that she was pondering all this in silence, he was actually talking out loud to himself, and she swore she heard him call her an ignorant bitch, but her own thoughts were so loud in her head that she wasn't sure.

Somehow she could not fathom that her boyfriend, Black, had just told her that he was not leaving his wife. That was all she heard him say. She missed all that other stuff he had said. So her mission the next day was to find his phone number, which wasn't hard since she knew many people who knew him. He was a neighborhood handyman, and had been for years. Candy reflected on how he had acquired the nickname "Black" as a kid. She was told that it was because he got in many fights and had many a black eye. It was kind of funny, because Black was a light-brown-skinned man. Anyway, the name just stuck throughout the years with his

85

neighborhood friends and family. Candy went down the street and lied by saying she needed to contact Black about a paint job to an older woman in the neighborhood who had used him for that kind of job before. The minute she got his phone number that day, she called his house, and his wife answered the phone.

"Hello. I'm calling to let you know that your husband and I have been seeing each other."

His wife was shocked at this news, and called her every kind of skank, ho, and bitch she could think of, and then slammed the phone down. Feeling triumphant, Candy believed that this would take care of his marriage, since he was afraid to tell his wife, and this would allow him to be her man without the distraction of that wife. So she went on down to the bar, figuring he would be relieved that she had helped him out of his marriage so he could be with her.

The door of the bar flew open and slammed into the wall behind it. Black came in with his eyes bulging out of his head and bloodshot red. He opened his mouth and the words came out like fire from a dragon. He cussed her out worse than anything imaginable in front of everyone that was there, and no one stopped him. He told the entire bar how he "fucked her in the dirt" in the forest and how he "fucked her on her front porch like the low down dog she was."

"And your pussy stank too, you rotten ho!" he shouted, and kept on shouting about how ignorant and stupid she was for about ten entire minutes. He went on and on and she sat there and didn't move. It looked like she wasn't even breathing, as if she had become inanimate, until she slowly reached her hand up from her lap onto the bar and grabbed her Budweiser bottle and slowly slid it down by her side, as if she was contemplating hitting him with it.

"Bitch! I wish you would hit me with that bottle! I'll beat you to death! You ever call my wife again, I'll kill you."

Candy just sat there with the bottle by her side, as if it were concealed. Finally, he stomped out of the bar and the place remained silent. About ten seconds later, some chuckling could be heard from the far end of the bar. Candy pulled the beer bottle up from her side and sat it back down on the bar, and she sat there for about five more minutes and said nothing. She could not believe he had dogged her like that. She finally got up and left as she tried to understand what she had done to make her boyfriend so mad that he would leave her like that.

So about a month later when a new guy who came into the bar with one of the regulars sat next to her and bought her a drink, she was back in the saddle again! Candy was thrilled that she had a new boyfriend, Ed. Ed took Candy to a short-stay, sleazy, crackhead motel the second time she saw him after they talked at the bar two nights in a row. And this time he gave her his number after the second trip to the sleazy motel. She never bothered to ask him why he didn't bring her to his place, and he didn't ask to go to hers either. The next day, she decided to call him before she headed down to the bar.

When she called, a woman answered. She figured that it had to be his sister or relative since he did give her his number. But the woman sounded disturbed as she asked

"Who is this?"

Candy said, "I'm Ed's girlfriend, who is this?"

The woman then rather calmly explained that she was Ed's girlfriend and that she was living there with him. Baffled, Candy told the woman that Ed gave her that phone number himself. The woman, who had obviously already dealt with this kind of madness from him before, just explained again that she was his woman and told Candy not to call there anymore.

Candy was crushed. That evening, she went to the bar and Ed did not show up. She asked one of his friends what happened to him and she was told that he had moved to another state. She was devastated for about ten minutes because she thought that answer was stupid. Then she forgot about him after knocking down another shot of vodka. What helped move her on was another woman who frequented the bar. This woman's husband was currently in prison, where he was apparently comfortable, since he kept going there over and over again.

The bar girlfriend whose husband lived in prison had received a letter from her husband that included a picture of a prison mate. The prison mate had the colossal nerve to include a note asking her to show his picture to some of her girlfriends so that they might contact him. "They won't be disappointed," he actually wrote at the end of his note. It's hard to imagine a man who decides he's not a disappointment while sitting in prison on his second stint for an armed robbery charge. However, the bar girlfriend passed this picture on to Candy knowing that she wouldn't be insulted at the gesture.

"He's cute!" Candy drunkenly slurred as she slid the picture into her purse. The bar girlfriend walked away knowing that Candy would probably send him a letter. *Mission accomplished*, she thought.

And send a letter she did, quite promptly, too, as she was starving for attention and desired to exclaim that she had a man. Being overweight most of her life had really taken a toll on her psyche and self-esteem, and had made her into a very defensive, needy person. Candy was an easy target for predators, and she never seemed learn much from these episodes. Instead, she usually concluded that something was wrong with any man who slighted her, or anyone else for that matter, and she would move on in scripted madness, realizing the same results almost every time.

Well this time it will be different, she thought, *since this man is in prison.* Shareef called her collect because Candy had put her phone number in the letter, and he instructed her to have phone sex with him every time he called. He was getting out of prison soon, and Candy told him she was living with her mother, so she could not put him up when he got out. Shareef contacted some of his relatives and found one who agreed to allow him to stay in a room of that relative's house.

When he got out, he was not thrilled with her look, but he figured she would do because he had no woman and he knew she would try to take care of him as much as she could. When he realized how much she liked to drink, he managed to talk her into moving into a tiny basement apartment where the rent was cheap enough for her to afford it. It was soon after that suggestion that he managed to get a job at a car wash, so Candy agreed, although the place smelled like mildew and was very dark and dank.

It wasn't long after they settled in there that Shareef began to not come home on some nights after work and would occasionally be missing for days. Candy refused to believe he had another girlfriend and would be furious until he came home, and then she'd be so glad he was there that she wouldn't be mad anymore. This went on for a while until she lost her job again. Shareef was so mad at her for losing her job that he called her all kinds of names, like "broke down bitch" and "ignorant ho." Candy cried and begged him to not leave. She promised she would get another job very soon, especially since it was mostly her money that paid the rent and bills while he mostly kept his money and only contributed when she told him she didn't have enough.

Candy found a bar in their neighborhood and had been frequenting the place soon after they moved to the area, so she was usually drunk by the time he got home, if he came home.

She took her first unemployment check and put some aside to go toward the rent, and then instead of going to the grocery store as she had intended when she stepped out the door, she made a turn at the first block and headed for the bar. She tied one on that night, and after a couple of hours she slithered back around the corner, took off all her clothes, and fell into the bed. Shareef had been in the bar before she got there, and someone told him when he got back that she had been there. One of the regular, older alcoholic bums that hung out there had told him that she was crying about not having enough money to pay the rent. He told Shareef he could help them out, but he wanted to know how much she meant to him. Shareef told this ancient alcoholic creature that she didn't mean shit to him, which everyone at that bar knew anyway from the way they had seen him act when she wasn't around. Shareef asked the grizzly, whiskered, drunken gargoyle what he had in mind. The man said that he would pay Shareef one hundred dollars if he let him go to his place to have sex with Candy. Shareef's mouth dropped open and he said, "What?" louder than he intended. And then he said it again, almost whispering; "What?"

That senior citizen son of an alligator had propositioned him to provide his woman for one hundred dollars. Shareef quickly realized he could probably get more, because this man was a beast, and probably wasn't getting much action to begin with. He wasn't smelling too good either, and his clothes were dirty. Shareef thought about how he hadn't slept with her in weeks, and he kept making excuses as to why he didn't want to have sex with her, the main reasons being that she was drunk, fat, and he had actually grown to despise her. He had some other young girl who was letting him sneak into her bedroom and spend the night sometimes, so he felt like he was straight.

"Well, Pops, I think I might allow this, but you'll have to pay me two hundred dollars."

The crusty drunk scratched the side of his head, poking his fingers underneath the nest of gray hair that was attached to it, and let out a sigh. Then he looked at him and said

"Okay."

They both left the bar and walked around the corner to the basement apartment where they knew she was probably laid out since she had clearly been smashed when she left earlier. Shareef directed the man to the bedroom and said he would be waiting in the living room. The man had already shown him the two hundred dollars, but he negotiated to actually hand it to him on his way out. He disappeared into the dark room behind the curtain they had hanging where a door used to be. The monstrous troll peeled his clothes off, exposing his skin to air for the first time in a couple of days. He pulled the covers back and saw she was naked already, which gave him much relief. He rolled her over and then rolled himself on top of her, pulling her legs open and up, grabbing her behind her knees, as both their stomachs impeded his penetration otherwise. And then he entered her and began pounding away, not even noticing whether she had even gained consciousness.

She had woken up during this event, wrapped her arms and legs around him, and just got right into the act. Candy didn't even realize she was being fucked by a gorilla. When he was done, he almost suffocated her as he lay on top of her with his deadweight and tried to catch his breath. He finally got up, grabbed his clothes, and walked out of the room to put his clothes on in the light.

"Damn, that was fast!" Shareef said as he watched this man put those filthy clothes back on.

Shareef was thinking that he would never put his dick in her ever again in his life now. The old man passed him the two hundred dollars that they had agreed upon and left.

Shareef decided to sleep on the couch because he could not even stomach the idea of lying in that bed after witnessing that scene. The thought of it made him want to vomit. He managed to fall asleep and it seemed like morning came immediately after he had eyes closed. Candy stepped through the curtain from the bedroom and asked him why he had gotten out of the bed.

Shareef was flabbergasted that she didn't even realize it wasn't him who had had sex with her. Candy walked into the bathroom and closed the door. He listened to her brushing her teeth and gargling, peeing, and then washing her hands. She came out of the bathroom smiling like she was in love because she believed that he had come home and made love to her that night. Projectile vomit shot out of his mouth before he even knew it had happened, and it landed on the snack stand that was next to the couch he slept on. Candy was shocked, and asked him if he was sick. Shareef said that he thought he had the flu as she grabbed some cloths to clean up the mess. She was walking on clouds and he was sickened by it. He went into the bathroom, took a shower, got dressed, and as he walked out the door, he waved at her. She smiled, feeling like she was in love, not knowing that it would be the last time he ever crossed that threshold.

Phantasmic Self

9

"I can't believe you did it!" Eric stormed away from Serita after seeing her doing what he had convinced her to do. She hadn't wanted to swap partners with their friends, the other couple that they hung around with, but after he had pleaded with her for a couple of nights, she decided she would do it because she loved him. She reluctantly found herself doing whatever he asked her to do quite often if she thought it would make him happy.

Eric and his friend had come up with the idea while they were watching a football game, drinking beer, and smoking weed one afternoon while their women were out shopping for some ribs to put on the grill. He had already fantasized about screwing his friend's woman anyway, so when his friend brought up the idea, it hadn't occurred to him that his friend was thinking the same thing about his woman. Eric was narrowly focused on what he wanted to do and how he could now possibly get his chance. The thought of it almost brought him to the point of drooling until his friend noticed the glazed-over look on Eric's face. He leaned over and punched him in the arm.

"Yo man! What you thinking about?"

"I was just trying come up with the right way to tell my girl."

They began talking about how it would be all right since they would all agree and that no one should be getting jealous or mad.

"It's just sex, man! It ain't like we falling in love with each other's woman or nothing" Eric exclaimed for himself as well as for his friend's benefit.

Once Eric said that, it seemed like a dose of reality seeped in, and he began to backpedal on the idea...

"Wait man...I don't know about this. I don't want to think about you fuckin' my woman."

His friend reminded him that he would be "fucking" his woman too— so they'd be even. He went on about how swingers handled this kind of thing and how plenty of people do this for fun. After more discussion, Eric was back on board and agreed that it would be something exciting to try.

By the time their women got back, they didn't say anything about their idea until after the food was cooked and after they ate. Serita had noticed that something was up because they were a little more quiet and subdued than usual, but she just chalked that up to the weed and beer. She had not indulged in any of that earlier, but decided to take a couple of pulls of weed after dinner. She knew she could not smoke any weed and go to the grocery store because she envisioned getting there and being stuck in the car in the parking lot, unable to face people in the store.

As they sat around the living room, Eric was busy raking seeds out of his weed using an old magazine he had lying around in his apartment. And finally, after the game went off, he leaned back and said to her that he and his friend were discussing a swap.

"You know…you with him and me with her."

At first she thought she had heard him wrong. Then Serita said she was totally against it as the other woman sat there and said nothing. She got up and walked into the kitchen, regretting ever hitting that joint. She felt like the weed was messing with her head, and for Eric to request such a thing meant that the weed must have been laced with angel dust or something.

Later that night, after the other couple left, Eric worked on her some more. He kept bringing it up all week long until she finally said she would do it. He had convinced her that it wasn't about love and that their love was so strong that this kind of recreational sex couldn't possibly come between them. Meanwhile, he could not stop thinking about screwing his friend's woman. He was anxious and thrilled at the idea of this new adventure.

And so, when the following Saturday arrived, and as usual, the four of them got together, the plan was set, and after some wine and weed, they retreated to separate rooms. Eric got up first and grabbed the hand of his friend's woman while she turned to look at her man, who she could tell was already in his perverted world by the look on his face.

Serita had heard from the friend's woman that her man was a freak, so she was bracing herself as well as trying to reconcile in her mind how not to be jealous about Eric being in the other room with his friend's woman. But when she got that image in her mind, and since he had gotten up so fast and grabbed her hand that way, she was a little miffed that he seemed so anxious to get with her, and she then decided she was going to go through with it and enjoy it.

Eric got his friend's woman into one of the two bedrooms and began kissing her and tearing her clothes off. They fell down onto the bed, and she was trying to unbuckle his pants when he suddenly rolled over and sat up. She looked at him puzzled, and asked him what was wrong. He only said that he'd be right back.

He walked out of the room and down to the other bedroom and poked his head through the door. When he saw Serita lying underneath his friend with her legs in the air and her hands locked onto the headboard of the bed while he was banging the shit out of her, he was furious. In his mind, she looked like she was enjoying it too much, and that pissed him off. They hadn't even noticed him peek in as he closed the door and went back to the other room and mechanically had sex with his friend's woman in anger. His friend's woman was completely disappointed and kept asking Eric what was wrong, but he said nothing. He had ended up feeling like having sex with his friends woman was retribution for Serita letting his friend make love to her, which was how he saw it.

Serita knew something was terribly wrong when she emerged from the bedroom she had been in with his friend. She was on her way into the hallway bathroom when he walked past her without looking at her or saying anything to her. She went into the bathroom and began to tremble, and she started taking deep breaths to try and pull herself together. By the time she came out of the bathroom, the other couple had left.

Serita went down the stairs and into the living room where Eric was and sat down next to him and he immediately got up and walked into the kitchen, saying nothing. She sat there and began to cry because he was visibly mad, and he began stomping back and forth from the kitchen to the living room, picking up glasses they had used earlier to drink wine and straightening up the living room as if she wasn't sitting there. He brushed past her as she headed for the kitchen to tell him she would clean up and still he said nothing and wouldn't look at her. Finally he sat down on the couch, and she followed. He glanced over at her, and then back to the TV.

"I can't even look at you! How could you do it?"

"What? It was your idea! I only did it because you insisted that we do this swap thing. I didn't even want to do it."

"Well you didn't have to get all into it like that! Damn legs all in the air! You really enjoyed yourself, huh bitch?"

She was devastated. Eric told her how he had changed his mind when he got in the room with his friend's woman and had come down to the other bedroom to tell them, only to find them already in the act. He completely blamed her for the whole thing because he felt that she had jumped into it too fast, while he had changed his mind. She felt so confused by the whole thing that she got her things and left his apartment. She had her own place, and usually stayed at his apartment on the weekends, but she could not stay there with this turmoil in the air. He didn't try to stop her from leaving either, which made her cry even more as she got into her car.

Serita was so enamored with Eric that she would do just about anything he wanted her to do. She knew it was wrong for her to be so pliable for him because he knew she was, and she could feel his selfish manipulation more and more. Yet, she could not imagine being without him for some reason. She kept telling herself that she had a good man who had been enrolled in the university just like she was, although he had dropped out after his freshman year. He left school, but not the campus area, and she was too young to realize how odd it was for him to be twenty-nine years old and still living in that off-campus area without being in any way connected to the school any more other than through the women he craved. His friend was almost just like him, except he had kept enrolling in school off and on over the years. Eric continuously said that he planned on going back and getting his degree, and she believed him, but he hadn't made any visible effort toward it during the entire year that she had been with him. Even though he managed to stay employed, he kept hanging around drug dealers and parasitic men who were about nothing, as if he needed them around him so he could feel bigger and better than someone. This was very bothersome to her, but she also saw him as being better than them, and she believed that Eric would eventually extricate this riffraff from his circle and marry her one day.

She cried herself to sleep that night after repeating to herself that it would all be better tomorrow once he calmed down about the whole thing. Eric polished off a bottle of wine which seemed to relax him, and he was able to climb the stairs to his bedroom and pass out across his bed that night. And the next morning he woke up and reached for Serita, who was not there. He lay there and thought about how she loved him very much, and how he liked having her around, so he decided to call her.

The entire event put a wrinkle in their friendship with the other couple, and after Eric was reminded over and over again by his friend how he had agreed and that he had screwed his woman too, he finally decided to relax about it. But the couples never visited again after that. He did still go out with his friend on occasion though, especially to pick up weed or stop at the strip club.

And then one night, it happened. He and his friend stopped by their regular drug dealer's apartment and he had more people over than usual. The drug dealer said it was his partner's birthday, and they were celebrating. The drug dealer told them to stick around and have some drinks, and they did, along with some weed, cocaine (which could have been meth for all they knew), and more liquor. They were wasted after a couple of hours, and neither one of them could drive. This seemed to be the case with quite a few people who were there, and somehow Eric ended up in a bedroom, sprawled out across a bed. In his drunken, drugged out stupor, it all seemed surreal as some guy came into the room and proceeded to rolled him over as he lay on the bed. He then unbuckled Eric's pants and began sucking his dick with a vengeance. Eric didn't stop him, and he felt his penis swell so tightly he thought it would explode, and explode he did, right into this man's mouth as he kept right at it, swallowing Eric's salty flow and slobbering it all over his face and the hand that held on to Eric's appendage. Eric was trying to reconcile what had just happened when he felt himself being rolled back over onto his stomach and he felt his pants being yanked down, and he felt something hard and hot enter his anus in one movement, slow and steady. He wanted to yell out because the pain was unbelievable at first. But he didn't yell. He didn't stop what was happening to him.

The man was relentless as he lay on top of Eric's back. Eric thought he was paralyzed, because he didn't fight as this man pulled his legs apart and sunk deeper into his asshole. This was something

96

he wrestled with in his head from that time on—whether he had really been paralyzed, or if he had just laid there. He felt the man's penis seem to snap the ejaculation up into his colon, and then he slid out, stood up, picked up a part of the bedspread and wiped his penis off, put his pants back on, and left the room, just like that.

Even if he wanted to kill the man or accuse him of rape, he wasn't sure he could even identify him. He was so drunk and high that he never even got a good look at the guy. Eric pulled his pants up and rolled over on his back. He felt sticky wetness drooling out of his ass, and he wanted to get up to see if it was blood, because he was now feeling some stinging pain from the surprising assault on his asshole. He lay there and was afraid to move, afraid to face anyone. He wondered if anyone knew.

It wasn't long before Eric's friend came into the room and told him he had passed out on the couch in the living room and he asked Eric how he ended up back there in the bedroom.

"What you mean, man?" he snapped.

"Calm down, man. I was just wondering what happened. I don't even remember how I ended up on the couch. Last thing I remember was that I was drinking shots of Hennessey in the kitchen."

Eric decided that his friend probably knew nothing about what had happened in that room, so he tried to act normally. But he still wondered who it was who had taken advantage of him. *Did he really take advantage?* This thought continued through his mind for days, months, years.

They left that place, and once Eric got to his apartment, he looked at his cell phone and saw all the missed calls from Serita. He was still stunned about the events of the night before, and all he could think about was sitting in a hot bath and soaking…and that's what he did. He had turned his cell phone off when they got to that place and he decided not to turn it on just yet. He had to collect his thoughts.

He never spoke of the events of that night with his friend or Serita. But he had a nagging urge to go back to that apartment to try to find out who had done that to him. So a couple of weeks later, he went there by himself, and the drug dealer let him in. They sat around drinking beer for a while and smoked a couple of joints. Soon after, the doorbell rang and it was a couple of other guys. They broke out the powder, and a couple of them disappeared into the kitchen to cook some rock for them to smoke. Eric wasn't into smoking crack, but he would sniff the powder. He asked if it was cocaine or meth and they all said it was cocaine, but he was suspicious. After a while, one of the guys called him into the back. Eric tried not to look anxious because he suspected that this was the guy who had fucked him mercilessly. He told himself that he had to confront this man for doing that to him as he walked back to that room. Eric stepped into the bedroom.

"You shouldn't have done that to me! I'm not gay man!"

"Sheeeet… neither am I" the guy plainly said. "It's just about sex bruh" and he reached for Eric's pants, unbuttoned, and unzipped them and pulled them down, dropped to his knees, and began to lick Eric's dick like a lollipop.

Eric pushed the guy back and said, "No, this time I am going to do you!"

The guy took his pants off with no argument, laid on his back, and raised his legs so that his feet were over his head, which caused his asshole to be exposed like a bull's eye. He climbed on top of the guy, and the thought flashed through his head that he didn't even know the guy's name. He pushed hard into this guy and fucked him like he would if he were having sex with a woman. After he splashed all he had up into that man, he pulled out ever so slowly and noticed he had shit on his dick. The guy told him to go wash up because he stunk. Eric wiped himself with the bedspread just like that guy did before and pulled his pants up. It was at this point that he realized he should have used a condom.

Well, Eric didn't go back to this place for a while after that, but he thought about it frequently. What he did do was convince Serita to allow him to have anal sex with her. At first, she was totally against it, and could not understand what brought this new urge on. In the back of her mind, she thought *Was he down low?* But she just refused to believe it. As he worked on her to allow it, she rationalized that he always wanted to try something freaky, and she had heard people say that women had to do what their men wanted to please them sexually or they would go elsewhere to be satisfied. She decided to let him try it and at first, it hurt her so badly that she didn't think she could let him do it again. She felt that it was nasty, and she was mad because after he would do that, he would try to put

98

his shitty dick in her vagina. All she could think about were the germs and infections he would be pumping up into her. After a few more times and some Vaseline, she finally got used to it, as he wanted to do it more often as time went on. She never enjoyed it, though.

What Serita didn't know was that Eric had begun to occasionally go back to that drug dealer's apartment and engage in down low sex with men. What she did know, months after he convinced her to let him wreck her anus, was that she didn't feel very well a lot of the time.

So she made an appointment to see her gynecologist, and as she sat there waiting, she wondered if she would throw up once she got into the doctor's office. She didn't really feel well as it was, but that was not why she was there. She believed that her anal sphincter muscle was damaged. She had been embarrassed a few times when loud flatulence unexpectedly escaped her in public and people turned and looked at her disgustedly.

The receptionist called Serita's name and she started forward in her seat. The receptionist asked for her insurance card and her co-pay, and then told her to sit back down.

Serita really did not want to be there in that office waiting and waiting as if she had nothing else in life to do— as if her time was not important. She felt she was at their mercy, as if she was at a sentencing in court. Sitting there waiting and waiting, she skimmed through two magazines as she tried to take her mind off of her suspicions. She listened to the nurses and office staff having a discussion behind the window of the reception area and she began to wonder if they remembered that she was there. *How rude was it to make an appointment with people, only to have them sit in their waiting room for hours,* she was thinking, but it hadn't been hours— it had only been thirty minutes. She felt like a hostage trapped in a doctor's waiting room, waiting to be tortured.

She was finally called into the examining room and the doctor had his nurse draw blood for lab work. She advised Serita to discontinue the anal sex because her sphincter muscle was torn. The doctor also told her to stop having sex without a condom with her boyfriend because of the discussion they'd had about how he all of a sudden wanted to have anal sex, especially when she revealed that

Struck By Lightning

she didn't really feel well for a few months after they started doing that. The doctor told her that women need to follow their instincts.

Serita knew these things about instinct and insisting that Eric wear a condom, but somehow she was too afraid to ask him if he was having down low sex. She was afraid to not allow him to have the kind of sex he wanted with her. She didn't want him to leave her. She wondered how she could possibly tell him he had to wear a condom with her after all this time.

"Yeast! I'll tell him I have a yeast infection."

~~~~~~

Eric didn't even show up for Serita's funeral. Her family had threatened to kill him, and her mother wanted to seriously press charges on him for murder by deceit. Once Serita told her family that she had full blown AIDS, they interrogated her, and then her brothers went after him. They believed that he knew he had HIV and still had unprotected sex with her regardless, but he actually did not know he was carrying the virus until she told him that she had AIDS. He had not contracted AIDS, and at first he tried to blame her, although he clearly knew that he was the one who engaged in risky sex with multiple partners in meth-induced madness at his drug dealer's apartment many, many times. She hadn't had sex with anyone other than him for more than a year—the entire time she was with him except that one episode when he convinced her to have sex with his friend in that swap deal. Those friends got tested too after learning about her condition, but neither of them had the virus. Eric had to admit to himself that he had contracted it in his escapades at the drug dealer's place, yet he was unapologetic as she drifted away from him and got sicker over time. He selfishly continued on in his down low lifestyle, recklessly.

Serita loved him, and that was the thought that traveled through her mind as her spirit began to release itself from the body it had been trapped in. And she slipped out of consciousness and into a peaceful place of eternal rest.

Thou Art Fruitful

10

"It's a damn shame, ain't it?" Pastor Jetson exclaimed as he passed Alison his phone number on a folded up piece of paper, which he had torn from the deceased person's program while riding to the cemetery.

Alison almost fell into the huge hole in the ground that the casket was being placed in by the heavy equipment used in that cemetery. She looked at the pastor as he handed her the paper, and she had no idea what the note could possibly say. When she opened it and saw his phone number, she was flabbergasted! She looked around to see if anyone saw him pass that paper to her, and it seemed that many did notice. As a matter of fact, many had noticed him looking at her well before Alison caught on.

She had never seen a burial like this before, and it seemed that almost nobody there expected that beautiful casket to be placed in an unmarked community grave. It seemed that somehow, no matter where Alison stood, Pastor Jetson was nearby, and when that crane pulled up to the burial site, he leaned over her shoulder from behind and whispered to Alison that it was a damn shame the family had spent so much on the casket and the beautiful programs, only to throw their mother into that community hole.

Alison just tried to play that entire scene off as she spun around to get away from him and that huge hole, which had what seemed like ten caskets already stacked up inside. She hurried back to the car she rode in, and was on her way to the repast at the church with her friends. One of her girlfriends turned to her and said,

"Are you crazy? Don't you know that man's wife was there?"

Alison was furious! She had had no part in the way that damn pastor had acted. "It wasn't me! He was flirting with me! He had the nerve to even give me his phone number!"

101

All of their mouths flopped open and one of her friends said she saw him do that. Then they all fell out laughing. Alison did not think it was funny at all, and decided she better not go to the repast, but since she wasn't driving, her drama-inducing girlfriends would not take her to her car. They laughed all the way back to the church about how Pastor Jetson's wife was gonna kick Alison's ass. And even though Alison laughed at the idea of that little old gray-haired woman kicking her ass, she wasn't laughing that hard. *One never knows*, she thought. The little old woman could have a gun in her purse for all she knew.

Pastor Jetson used to be a deacon at another church on the other side of town. The deacon board threw him out because he was married but had left his wife and moved in with his mistress, and he had had the nerve to bring his mistress to church while he still married to his wife. His wife was too humiliated to come there anymore, and she began going to another church. Once they told him he could no longer be a deacon because of his behavior, he got mad and told them he was leaving that church because he was going to be ordained as a minister and become the head of his own church.

Pastor Jetson had two children with his wife who were grown and had moved away for college. There were others too, because he had three children by two other women prior to his marrying his wife, but they were older and living in other states. And then there was the younger child, who was just ten years old, he had had by another mistress. That woman was considerably young even by his standards being that she was in her twenties when they got together. He usually went for women who were in their mid-thirties to early forties because he had no patience for the younger sort. He liked a challenge, and he also felt empowered by spreading his seed to needy women whose clocks were ticking, and that was the age range which he knew he could oblige easily.

Pastor Jetson was a good-looking man. He was a tall, chocolate-brown-skinned man with a nice head of hair which he kept groomed very well. He jogged in the mornings and ate well to stay in shape. He had a deep baritone voice that was so appealing to so many women, many of them came to church just to hear his voice instead of being there to hear what he was actually saying. And he knew this. So he did have a following, and when he left the church where the deacon board fired him, many of the women followed him to his new church, where he managed to become assistant pastor. Before he wedged his way into the new church, he dropped the mistress and got back together with his wife, who allowed him to move back into their house.

His wife had been through this many times, and it seemed that the older she got, the younger he looked. She couldn't figure it out why she was gradually looking so haggardly while he continued to look youthful. She figured that it had to be attributed to the depression that she was stuck in. And since she was too embarrassed to get help, she remained in a state of semi-catatonic consciousness. Some who knew her well thought Pastor Jetson was cruel to allow his wife to sheepishly stand by while he was blatantly flirtatious. Some were actually jealous of her, because they felt that no matter what he did outside of their relationship, he still went home to her in the end.

And so it was here at this church where he was assistant pastor and where the funeral was held for Alison's friend's mother that she encountered Pastor Jetson. Alison was particularly uncomfortable with his attention for more than just the fact that he was married and the fact that he boldly flirted with her, regardless of who saw him. The problem was that she realized she was actually turned on by him. There was something about him that was scary to her. She seemed to always be attracted to thug types, and this pastor fit that description. She got a strong sense from him as he spoke to her in his confident, willful, and passionate way, when he explained why he wanted her to call him as he caught her in the hallway outside of the dining hall of the church. He was saying something about a church bazaar, but his mannerism and vibe was saying something totally different.

Alison told him she couldn't and wouldn't and backed away from this church gangsta, through the door, and into the dining hall. When she turned around, she saw his wife sitting at the first table there, staring at her. Alison just turned to the right and found a table on the other side of the room where her friends were sitting. They were cracking up about the whole thing, but it wasn't funny at all. Alison was really annoyed by now and wanted to leave. She made a mental note to never ride with these clowns anywhere ever again.

When Alison finally got home, there was a message for her on her answering machine. To her shock and amazement, it was him! Pastor Jetson had managed to get her phone number from someone at the service, and he had called her. He threatened to call her back later. Alison fell back onto her bed and just stared at the ceiling as she wondered what she ever did in life to deserve this madness. And then she wondered just how strong she was, because contemplation kept floating through her mind. There was something about his pursuit that was getting her all hot and bothered inside.

The next day, Pastor Jetson did call Alison again and his deep voice seemed to make her go into a trance as he overpowered her through conversation on the phone, and he managed to get her to agree to go to a basketball game with him. He explained that his wife did not like basketball and that his brother had extra tickets. Alison told him that it was wrong for him to be calling her, but he cut her off at every protest to tell her how "all right" it was because of his "unique" relationship and ministry.

"Did he say ministry?" Alison mumbled under her breath in puzzlement as he continued to talk about picking her up.

So when she stepped outside on the night of the basketball game to be picked up by Pastor Jetson, she could not believe that this man was driving one of those old land yachts—an old caddy that stretched from almost one end of her block to the other. It was in good condition too, a gleaming metallic green on the outside with creamy white leather seats on the inside. It was like riding down the street in a living room it was so roomy and comfortable. Being that kind of comfortable in his car sent a chill up Alison's spine. She was thinking that this man probably used to wear a Jheri curl and slither his way through women in the church like a hot knife through butter. She was imagining him dripping with "soul glow" like in the movie "Coming to America," and she laughed to herself, which caught his attention.

"What you laughing about?" he said as he drove onto the highway toward the arena. This man was so vain. He had not a shred of insecurity in him. It was greed and validation through women that ruled his world Alison figured.

"What do you want with me?" she blurted out as they made their way down the highway.

"I feel a strong connection to you— it's very spiritual and I can't ignore it." He glanced over at her, from her head to her feet.

104

He went on to say that he knew she felt it too. This caused Alison to pause, because she had to wonder if she really did feel it. His rap was so confident and confusing that by the time they pulled into the parking lot of the arena, she didn't know whether she was in love or lust or hated his ass.

Pastor Jetson could only reflect on one time that he encountered a woman who had resisted him, which had been a real blow to his ego. Although it didn't stay deflated for long, he was severely insulted, especially after he found one of the women he was seeing a few years ago on the floor of her living room—legs spread eagle—with another woman's head in her crotch.

He had a key to this woman's apartment and had just showed up one day because she had been so callous to him and had even told him not to come by that night. He was not used to rejection, and she had rejected him on many an occasion, which had intrigued him at first, because she had held out on him for so long. He wasn't a cheap man either and knew how to wine and dine a woman, so he could not understand this woman who was resisting him because he simply felt that he was irresistible. So when she told him on this particular day to not come by, she hadn't let him come by the night before either. And the night before that, she had told him she would be out with friends. He was furious because they had been on a few dates already, and usually what that meant to him was that she was hooked.

When he went there that day, he hadn't even expected to find her at home. He was mad and had planned to leave her key with a note to tell her that he was through with her. Instead, he was through, but not for the reason he had thought he would be. He could not get past the image of that woman's head in his woman's crotch. He walked out the door and never looked back.

Pastor Jetson and Alison had fun at the basketball game. She actually forgot he was a pastor while she was there with him and called him by his first name, James. He went to get some popcorn, hotdogs, and soda from the concession stand, and once he made it out to the stairs, his brother leaned over to Alison and told her how disgusted he was with his brother. Alison wasn't prepared to hear that, she was enjoying her denial and having fun at the game. She couldn't understand why his brother felt compelled to let her know that at this time. She looked at him and just shrugged her shoulders.

He went on to say how he thought it was terrible how he had so many women all the time.

The statement made by Pastor Jetson's brother caught Alison's attention, although she tried to ignore it. She thought she was the only potential mistress being pursued in this equation. Pastor Jetson came back, sat down, and they continued to enjoy the game. Afterward, they all agreed to meet at Mr. Gee's Lounge. Alison didn't tell Pastor Jetson what his brother had said, but she was clearly feeling a little more grounded, instead of having her head in the clouds. Pastor Jetson noticed the difference, too, as he drove from the arena. They went inside the lounge and he ordered drinks for them. He then asked her if he could take her home. Alison turned to him and said, "No, I have called a friend to pick me up."

"What? Why did you do that?"

"You know, you almost swept me off my feet. But I've had a chance to get a grip on reality".

Pastor Jetson tried to interject, but she kept talking. She told him that she had no idea why he was such a whore, but she could not be a part of it.

He sat back and looked at her face and realized that she was serious. And he was skilled at reading people and knew that there was no turning this situation around with her. He leaned forward and finished his drink and turned to her smiling.

"Don't you realize that women make up 90 percent of my congregation? These women are in need of ministering. I am providing them with what they need and they love me for it."

As Alison rode home, she felt triumphant. She had come so close to being another notch in his belt. But the blessing of choice had kicked in. "Thank God!"

106

Epilogue

People are living in legacies of dysfunction and we have to do better. We have to collectively make an effort to lift each other up— encourage high self-esteem, self-respect, self-love.

I mean, it's not all bad… Or is it? I actually do know some people who have made their relationships and marriages work. (The key word here is *work*.) It takes effort for those involved to make their relationships work, and it really helps if both know the other's goals in life so that they can be an asset to each other, even if not fully invested in the other's idea. In other words, don't stand in the way of each other's dreams, even when it isn't your dream. That's just my one-and-a-half cents…

Does anyone actually expect relationships to be like a fairy tale? For the sun to come out and brighten up the day and for everything to be good all the time? For a knight in shining armor to arrive in the nick of time to sweep the damsel in distress off her feet and then he ends up being the man who cares for her every need?

Now really! Let reality roll in! Those damn fairy tales have ruined many a psyche for many women in my opinion. Kiss a frog and he turns into a prince… I've seen many a "frog" lying around on the sidewalks of inner cities. If it was just a matter of picking one of them up (and dusting him off in a disinfectant shower while wearing a hazmat suit) and then laying a kiss on him to magically make the man of our dreams appear, (a working, viable man that is…) we wouldn't be having this kind of discussion.

Nothing wrong with a fantasy when it has a shred of reality in it… Those kinds of dreams give us something to aspire to. However, we have to realize that our dreams shouldn't include turning a well-anchored sloth into a prince with a work ethic or a June Cleaver/super housewife/homemaker. You have to have something to work with…

It's hard to acknowledge our failings— denial seems easier. Yet denial is our worst enemy because it allows us to remain in our madness. It's amazing to me that sometimes while wallowing in madness and dysfunction and shrouded in denial, we can actually point out the madness of others, as if we aren't living the same lunacy and nightmare in our own relationships.

I can only hope that we manage to do better by teaching our younger folks coming behind us to do better. If we haven't managed to be the example, we can at least acknowledge our shortcomings and try to convey to those behind us that they don't have to make the same mistakes. Some of us have already been down some dark and bumpy roads, and it wasn't pretty.

Now of course, many would have to learn the hard-headed lessons. I've been known to have a few lumps and scrapes myself. But the lessons are out there to be learned. Being resistant to these lessons might mean that it will take longer to learn them, and result in remaining in the madness of dysfunction until they are learned and accepted.

And then there's the matter of respect.

If we manage to respect each other, maybe we wouldn't be so selfish in our actions that affect others. What ever happened to respect anyway? As a child growing up (many moons ago), we learned very early about respect. Never interject into an adult conversation as a child. Never talk back or be disrespectful to an adult. We were instructed to bring any issues we had with adults to our parents... and believe me, they would take care of it. We learned about having manners and looking out for one another. We learned to take pride in the place we lived. We learned early about the value of money through chores at home and earning an allowance. We learned about the value of education and most importantly, about giving honor to God by acknowledging our blessings.

I guess people have gotten tired, overwhelmed, misguided, befuddled, confused, and/or apathetic for a multitude of reasons. So it seems to me that it's going to be really tough to regain respect as a rule instead of as an exception. There are so many young people who don't even believe in or value the longevity of lives anymore, thus there is no respect for life. Murder became just a way of life in some areas and that is tremendously sad.

But respect can happen if we demand it. We have to demand it through our actions, by earning it and by teaching it. Those of us who have lived long enough and are blessed enough to be able to look back and reflect and say "Thank God, I made it through," should share their stories so that others can learn to do things differently when mistakes are made and to pick up some tools when things have worked out well. It's difficult though for those of us who have no frame of reference in the respect department. Some people grow up accepting disrespect in their lives because that's the kind of environment they have lived in.

The bottom line is that none of us should ever accept being mistreated and disrespected for the sake of being in a relationship. The person who is doing the mistreating may have a psychosis that is well beyond our expertise to fix. When things are spiraling downward, at some point a decision has to be made to move on.

Where is the love?

Seems that long ago, love included sacrifice and long-term goals that included each other and family. It seems that there was more of an effort to achieve the family goal. I truly believe that we have to get away from the blame game of 'it's the woman's fault or "it's the man's fault." These games have placed us so far apart in our lives. There are just too many factors on both sides and outside, which have infiltrated our notion of love and family, to say that one gender is more at fault than the other.

It wasn't *that* long ago when I remember there was so much music that was all about love, and there were so many singers and groups who were romantic crooners.

Remember *The Ebonys, Temptations, Commodores, Blue Magic, Temprees, The Escorts, Enchantment, The Stylistics,* and The *Delphonics*? What ever happened to this kind of music, the kind that was all about a mood of falling in and out of love and romance? Now I hear lyrics such as "I'm into havin' sex / I'm not into makin' love" and all about "bitches and hoes" and whatnot. Lawd! And then seeing all these young girls, who are proud to be bitches and hoes, swinging their asses all up in the camera on BET and MTV, etc. Lawd, again!

Where are we headed?

More and more I hear men discussing the benefits of polygamy and how it is actually a fact for many women in some form or fashion, whether they want to admit it or not. And what's worse, some of these poly-amorous men are being supported by their multiple women, as if that were their occupations. There's something wrong with that picture.

So do we all just go it alone? Should male and female brothels become abundant and fertility clinics and sperm banks become our procreative norm?

Yet, after saying all that, I believe that in order to see change happen, women must make sacrifices in order to stop accepting *just any man* into her life—just for the sake of *having a man*. It's no longer a stigma to not be married. We have to raise the bar on the men we accept or they will never feel compelled to do better. This means that some of us will most likely have to endure going it alone as many already do. And many times, going it alone beats the alternative, especially when that alternative is detrimental to your personal well-being and that of your children.

I believe that we have arrived at this point due to the abuse of power ("Absolute power corrupts, absolutely!"). Women have adapted out of necessity because when men had all the power in their roles as heads of households, many men abused their positions. Women were traditionally trained to be homemakers and housewives. Being totally dependent created a situation in which many men decided they could pretty much live as they pleased— with mistresses on the side, or being outright physically and mentally abusive for any number of reasons. Women realized that in order to not feel trapped in lives of despair there was a need to have some control over their destinies. Maybe the pendulum of equality has swung too far from one side to the other, but it had to happen. Nevertheless, a balance needs to be achieved that we can all live with... somehow.

Men have to make sacrifices too, which include being more discerning about who they choose to mate with. Men have to start using more of the brain in the head on their shoulders because the world has become a more complex and competitive place. Dropping seed all over town indiscriminately is simply irresponsible. Deciding that birth control is a woman's responsibility is equally irresponsible. Being irresponsible means being left behind in many cases. It can certainly mean tons of child support payments and no driver's licenses, and jail time if you decide not to pay up.

Okay, it's not all gloom and doom either, because some people do actually get it right, make the effort to get it right, have the right karma, are in the right place/right time, all that. I am always happy to see that, because it's a reminder that it can happen. We all have to do some self-analysis, and then make choices in our lives that promote our ideas and goals.

Let's have some good goals and turn the bleakness of our relationships around. It involves give and take, compromise and compassion, empathy and caring, and love. We can do it! We should do it! Let's do it!

Made in the USA
Charleston, SC
15 July 2014